The Death of Us

ALICE KUIPERS

Harper*Trophy* Canada

The Death of Us
Copyright © 2014 by Alice Kuipers.
All rights reserved.

Published by Harper*Trophy*Canada™, an imprint of
HarperCollins Publishers Ltd.

First edition

HarperCollins books may be purchased for educational, business, or
sales promotional use through our Special Markets Department.

HarperCollins Publishers Ltd
2 Bloor Street East, 20th Floor
Toronto, Ontario, Canada
M4W 1A8

www.harpercollins.ca

Library and Archives Canada Cataloguing in Publication
information is available upon request.

ISBN 978-1-44342-410-3

Printed and bound in the United States of America
RRD 9 8 7 6 5 4 3 2 1

For Shatille, who is bright, brilliant and beautiful

ONE

JULY 31ST

Kurt

I lean against a tree at the back of the yard, the night around me like black water. I check my pockets for cigarettes but I'm out. Xander's party is going strong—beer, hot dogs, parents away.

Xander surfaces from the house. Prairie-dog slim and tall. Fast too. He makes sure people have beers, joins the group of guys near me. I drift over. Listen in. They're talking about girls. About Ivy. Sure, they all want her. Blonde, sexy. Flips her hair over her shoulder when she wants me to kiss her. She's just out of reach. Just something. The girl everyone watches on a stage. Can't help it.

One of the guys, Greg, asks, "So Ivy's coming?"

Xander says, "She's bringing Callie."

"Callie's hot too. Not like Ivy, but worth it." Hankering for details from me, he adds, "Man, I bet Ivy's wild."

There's a scream inside the house. A girl — Angel I think her name is, long black hair, not angelic from what I've heard — stumbles out. She's holding up her phone, yelling my name. "Kurt!"

Xander grabs her before she can get to me.

Slick-sheen sweat over Angel's cheeks. She waves her phone. "There's been an accident. Look, Dustin sent this. He didn't realize . . . but look."

I'm closer now. Too close. On her phone is a photo of the main traffic bridge, but something's wrong. A section of the barrier is missing. I let out a low whistle. "Man, someone hit that hard."

She flicks to the next image. "I'm right, aren't I?"

Then I see why she's so stressed out. Police and firefighters are pulling a car out of the river. The car is smashed up but not beyond recognition.

It's Ivy's car.

My stomach roils.

It's *Ivy's* car.

Angel is frantic.

Oh man, I think. *Callie.*

FOURTEEN DAYS EARLIER

Ivy

We arrive at the edge of Edenville. Kevin has old-person music playing from his phone through the car stereo, his hand is on Mom's leg and the two of them are singing. I stare out the window and hum along. The sun is shining and the wide road is an invitation. The houses in this neighbourhood are quaint, wooden, totally charming.

Soon Kevin pulls into the alleyway at the back of his house. Same house, same muddy alleyway, same everything. The memories rush back. Three years since we lived here and everything's exactly the same.

Except me. I'm different.

Mom turns back to me with a sunny smile. "You okay?"

"Sure, why wouldn't I be?"

She nuzzles into Kevin. There's honestly no way to be nice about it. He's gross. Balding, eager, too fat in the cheeks, in the tummy, in the butt.

"Up we go," he says. He's always saying things that don't make any sense. Up where? Mom thinks listening to a man is important. Maybe one day one of her boyfriends will say something worth listening to. I smile at my own joke and open the car door, glancing at Callie's house, two yards over. I remember arriving here the first time, seeing her sitting in the tree, legs dangling. Her red hair held up with a pen. She scowled at me like an angry cat.

"What are you up to?" I asked her.

"Nothing." She chewed her thumbnail.

I said, "Come down and show me around. I'm new."

She narrowed her eyes, weighed me up in that way she has and scrambled down the tree. Three years ago feels like three minutes.

Kevin and Mom are giggling together, getting out of the car. He swoops her into his arms and they do the honeymoon thing — over the threshold, him hauling around his prize, her laughing throatily.

My heart flies back to Kansas — Dorothy-style. I'm wrapped up in Diego and it's me laughing throatily against his chest, him kissing me, then kissing me harder.

I linger on an image of Diego jumping off the stage and lightly tapping the ends of his drumsticks down my chest. *Hell yeah, Ivy.* But we're not in Kansas anymore. I smooth my hair and brush imaginary dust from my white shirtdress. I'm going to see if Callie still lives here — shiny-penny Callie in the bank account of my life.

Callie

I get it, I do. They have a baby now and they've done their part: what a successful, balanced teenager they've created.

I don't take drugs. *Check.*

I don't drink. *Check.*

I don't go to wild parties. *Check.*

Okay, I have a couple extra piercings in my

right ear that Mom hates. And I've dyed my hair black, which Dad moans about. And he definitely can't understand why the dark-blue nail polish, with one green nail on the fourth finger of each hand. I've told him there's nothing to understand.

Still, I keep my room tidy. *Check*.

I get my homework in on time. *Check*.

I'll get into any university I want, probably. *Check*.

I'm perfectly bone-crushingly normal. *Check. Check. Check.*

If only I didn't feel like I do right now around my parents, we could all just get along like we used to.

I slump over the kitchen table. Mom has Cosmo strapped to her in the sling and she's doing that foot-shift thing that mothers do. Right foot, left foot, right foot, left foot, baby swaying. He's staring up at her, she's staring down at him. Mother and child, mother and child, and I shouldn't care, really, but there's this jagged feeling in my chest that I can't make go away. I'm pretty sure I should be delighted with a baby in the house; I truly thought I would be. Babies are cute. And he *is* cute. I know I should be over it. I'm sixteen and I should be able to deal with my mom having a new baby.

I pick at my nail polish, flip through my phone. Rebecca's put up a hilarious video of her holding a doll. "BABY!" her voice-over yells. I snort.

Mom glances over. "What's that?"

"Doesn't matter."

"Could you turn it down? Cosmo's just about to fall asleep. I might, actually, get some work done today."

The video replays so Rebecca's voice comes through loud, loud, loud. "BABY! BABY! BABY!"

"Callie, turn it down. Anyway, you shouldn't be using the phone at the table."

There's no one at the table with me. The phone rule doesn't apply, surely, when I'm the only one sitting here. But Mom looks too exhausted for me to bother arguing. I slide the phone away obediently. Seems the only time Mom has anything to say to me now, we're talking either about Cosmo or about things I should be doing differently.

Silky light tumbles all over the cluttered living room, catching on the colourful baby seat, packets of diapers, toys and musical instruments. Mom's latest picture-book manuscript is spread over the bench by the window. Her glorious illustrations come alive in the sun.

She sees me looking. "Nearly done. I just have to go over these pages now he's sleeping." She strokes the baby's head tenderly. "Then we're going to see the twins for coffee at three. Want to come?"

"And hang out with a bunch of babies? No thanks."

"Okay, Callie. Well, don't waste your day. You've had weeks off already and you still haven't got a job."

"I've *tried*."

"You haven't been to any of the hotels yet, like I suggested."

"I *have*. I told you, I went yesterday. It's not as easy as you think, Mom. I've dropped off my resumés in, like, loads of places. No one's calling."

"Come on, Callie. You shouldn't need me to tell you this—use a little initiative. Go back to the same places. Offer to come anytime they need. Make yourself available. You need a job—"

"It's like you want me out of the house."

"Honey, that's not it at all."

Dad comes into the room and heads straight for her. He's a bearded guy with glasses and a selection of similarly checked shirts and blue jeans, and he's the owner of a big booming voice. He has a love of beautiful things, theatre, Greek epics and my mother. He kisses her hard on the mouth, sweeping her backward in his arms. She laughs and swats him away.

"Honey, you're squashing the baby."

Cosmo gurgles. Mom pretends to be mad at Dad for waking him, rolling her eyes, sighing, but she isn't really mad. I know I should be grateful, or whatever, that my parents are so obsessed with each other. I reach for my phone and read a couple stupid posts. Mom starts singing to Cosmo. I imagine she sang the same songs to me a thousand years ago.

Dad interrupts my pity party. "Busy day, Calliope?"

I shake my head and lean back in my seat, wiping the toast crumbs from my mouth. "I'm just finishing edits on my article. Then, I dunno."

"What's Rebecca doing?"

"I told you already. She's away with her dad, camping."

"So you can't message each other a million times a day?" He feigns horror by widening his eyes.

"She has Internet."

"In the bush? Good lord, what's the world coming to?"

"It doesn't work all the time."

"What about your other friends. Oh, what's her name?" He snaps his fingers. "The flower girl."

"You mean Dahlia?"

"That's the one."

"Europe with Liona until school starts. Tilly and family are away too."

"I know. They're at their cabin? See? I listen." He hooks a thumb in his belt-loop. "Did you read *Bonjour Tristesse* again yet?"

Every summer I reread it. As the sun falls through the window like this and the smell of sunscreen and cut grass sneaks through the open door, I find myself wanting to experience the story of Cecile growing up all over again. The first time I read it, when I was thirteen, the darkness of how Cecile manipulates her father's girlfriends, the mess of it, the suicide, all of it, made me feel more alive. Françoise Sagan wrote the novel when she was only eighteen—two years older than I am now. Each year I read it and hope that maybe, maybe this will be the year I actually start to write fiction. My phone buzzes in my hand.

The text is from Kurt Hartnett: **Done the piece?**

He's the editor of *Flat Earth Theory*, the school zine. He's lining it up for the start of the school year, and he wants an article on the name of our team: Redmen. Is it heinous and racist, or a tradition? It's interesting to figure out how to write the piece in a balanced way. The three people I interviewed got het up as soon as they started talking.

I have the article in front of me, printed out, while I noodle through with last-minute edits. I snap a photo of it and send the image to him with the words **Just about done**. I lean back a little farther, the front legs of my chair off the wooden floor.

"Careful not to fall, Callie," Mom says.

She's barely looking at me. How does she know?

Kurt texts: **Now, now, now!**

I orient the chair so its four feet are back on the ground and reply: **Take it easy!**

—**Wanna meet 2mr 2 talk it over?**

—**mebbe. Let's see if I finish it first. U know I wanna get it perfect.**

※

About four hours later, my copy of *Bonjour Tristesse*
lies open on the couch. I've been eating a peach
over the kitchen sink, the juice dripping down
my chin, my fingers sticky, the peach perfectly
sweet and delicious. As I wash my hands, I'm busy
thinking about the day ahead: I might wander to the
gallery and talk to Kurt, who works there, about
the article. I might try and catch Tilly online, or
even Dahlia, whatever time zone she's in, although
Mom'll give me a hard time for chatting with
friends, since I haven't got around to dropping
off my resumé anywhere yet today. Instead, I got
caught up with the article; changing one line made
me change another, and then another. I suppose I
could go and do the resumé thing now.

Mom is upstairs, cooing at Cosmo. Dad went
out a while ago: he has an office at the university. I
mention Dad because when the front door swings
open, I assume it's him. I don't even look up.

"Callie, you *do* still live here!"

I almost choke.

"It's been forever," she cries as I turn to face her.

I'm unable to speak because *Ivy Foulds* has
skimmed across my hallway, past the kitchen

counter that juts into our open-plan space, and grabbed me in a huge perfume-saturated hug. She smells just like she used to, vanilla with a hint of something deeper, a dark forest. Her hair is messy in my face and for a long moment I have to swallow the lump in my throat. I hug her hard. She's light-boned, fragile but strong, like a bird.

She pulls away and takes a good look at me. "Black hair? Cute. So? Did you, like, miss me so much? Can you believe I'm back? Uh, did you have a baby or something? What's with all the kiddie toys?"

"M-my baby brother . . . Cosmo," I manage to stammer.

She's standing less than a foot away. When we were thirteen, she was pretty. Now she's *stunning*, her platinum-blonde hair flat-ironed, her grey eyes the same silvery snakeskin pattern I always envied, her skin tanned and flawless, long arms and legs poking from a white shirtdress that looks expensive. I'm still shorter than her, chubbier than her, and I'm wearing my most comfortable, most untrendy black leggings and oversize tee.

"We got back, like, uh, now. I came straight over; the door was open. Oh, I hoped you'd be here!

Callie, we're going to have so much fun. We're going to rule Grade Eleven, just like we planned, remember?"

I remember, I want to say. *I remember how much it hurt when you left and didn't say goodbye.* I lean against the counter.

She says, "You wanna know what happened, right? I bet you wondered. Did you, like, stalk me online?"

"Um . . ."

"I'm not easy to find. I know. So retro, it's cool." She lowers her voice conspiratorially. "See, I'm not under my real name. I'm Kansas Pearl."

"I did look for you, course."

"There's so much I have to tell you. But first, *you*. How are you? How's everything? *Baby* brother? Where is he?"

"Upstairs. Wanna meet him?"

"Or you could come to Kevin's house and unpack with me. Remember? That's what we did last time."

"Your mom's back with Kevin?"

"Seems he's running things at the potash mine now. Big shot. Bought me this dress." She widens her arms to show it off.

"I've seen him around. He never said . . . Not that he'd think to tell me, I guess."

"So, will you come?"

"Unpack? Sure. Let me tell Mom."

"I can't believe you're still here," she says. "You look great. Beautiful, as always."

I laugh off her compliment. "Yeah, yeah."

"I really missed you." She reaches for my hand and squeezes it.

I squeeze back. "I came over with flowers the day after. Kevin answered the door and told me you'd gone."

"And now I'm here."

"You are." I find myself smiling.

She drops my hand. "It wasn't up to me, you know."

"I bet." Cosmo starts yelling upstairs. I say, "I'll text Mom later. She probably won't even notice. Come on, didn't you say you had unpacking to do?"

TWO

JULY 31ST

Kurt

Xander gets into his car and I slide into the passenger seat. He mutters, "Go, go."

People are streaming out like rats. One of the cheerleaders takes flash photo after flash photo of Xander's car. A gruesome online montage will follow. Sick. A group of girls press around Angel, gasping, crying. *Stop*, I want to shout, but I yell at Xander instead.

"Get moving, would you?"

Xander says nothing. He turns his key, hits the accelerator.

Outside, the quarterback rounds people up. Get them away. Good. Then I'm calculating the distance from the bridge to the river, the impact, the speed of the car. Party forgotten.

Xander doesn't speak. He's the guy you want beside you when you're stuck in a lifeboat. The guy you want with you when your plane crashes in the Amazon and everyone else is dead.

That word. Solid. Final. A flat, dull word punctuated at either end by the tongue. I've spoken out loud. *Dead*.

Xander says, "Come on, man. Give me something." His phone beeps. "Yep," he says, reading the text. He chucks the phone between us. I read the message: **St Mary's Hosp**. It's from that ER friend of his.

Xander takes a left too sharply, tense. Speeds through a red light and crosses the other bridge, the narrower one. I don't want to look at the main bridge, the one the car went off, but I crane my neck. The flash of police lights. Boats below. Four of them. I imagine her under water, struggling to breathe, trapped in the car's metal embrace.

Callie would like that image. Man, would she ever.

Xander hustles down a residential street at seventy K. Too fast. But go faster. Hurry. He's making a right on Main, past Callie's house. I see through the window, although I wish I hadn't, her baby brother, Cosmo. Held in someone's arms. Screaming.

FOURTEEN DAYS EARLIER

Ivy

"Still messy?" says Callie.

"Who, me?" We're in my bedroom, unpacking my clothes and trying to fit everything into a space that's still plastered with posters of boy bands we used to adore. Stuff is all over, clothes piled everywhere, magazines, my brand-new laptop — *thanks, Kevin* — eReader, old photographs. There's one of me and Callie. I hold it up.

It shows the two of us hugging like crazy,

beaming at the camera. For a moment, I'm there, Callie's hair splashing in my face, the smell of her shampoo and raspberry lip balm. Callie's dad took the shot just before we went for that walk.

I say, "God, we're gorgeous."

"Whatever." She smiles, though.

I show her a different photo of the two of us sunbathing in her yard, and say, "Your hair looks good your original colour, you know."

"You sound like my dad. I like it like this."

"At least let me paint your nails over."

"What, you don't like dark blue?"

"I like the colour but it's chipped."

"Now you really do sound like my dad." Callie looks out the window. "You can see my front door from here. Look, there's Mom and Cosmo. They're going for coffee with these baby twins. Mom's really into the whole baby thing."

"Is she?" I glance out. Her mom is pushing a stroller down the street, facing away from us. She walks like Callie—slightly stiffly, her shoulders up. She never liked me. She writes about love and compassion in her picture books, but I never saw much evidence of that. Maybe this time around I can convince her I'm a good person. I say, "What's Cosmo like? I wanna meet him."

"I dunno. He cries a lot."

"If you won't let me paint your nails, at least stop staring out the window and help me with this, will you?"

Callie stands beside me as we wrestle an extra clothing rod into the wardrobe. Once it's in place, we hang my dresses. She bends over to start unpacking the last of my gigantic suitcases and pulls out a dress with tiny straps. "Wow," she says. "It's like a spiderweb. Is it silk?"

"That old thing? Have it. I never wear it anymore. I wear white. Can't you tell?" I glance at the row of dresses we've just hung. All of them are white or cream.

"Really, I could have it? It's beautiful."

"Stuff weighs you down, right? Time to start over."

Callie says, "You sound a little sad."

My left shoulder lifts and drops. "Sorta."

"Come on, you can trust me," she says. "You know that."

"I was in love with this guy in Kansas City."

Something opens in me, like a hole where a tooth used to be. I probe it and feel the absence.

She says, "Kansas Pearl? You lived in Kansas City, then?"

"That's where we were for the last year. Before that, San Francisco—Mom even tried to fire it up with my dad. Online. Just for a few months. You can imagine how that worked out."

"Not good?"

"We don't have to pretend."

"Don't we?" Callie suddenly won't catch my eye.

"You never told, right?" I say. "Not Kevin? Not even your mom?"

"Course not."

"I knew you probably hadn't told Kevin or he wouldn't have us back." Callie was always loyal— you can see it in her, like you can in a horse. I mean that in the best way—a fine, loyal horse. It makes me want to do something for her, like fix her hair, or get her some decent clothes. There aren't so many loyal people on this earth.

"Are you happy to be in Edenville?" she asks.

"I didn't want to leave Kansas. Understatement. I—" I touch my chest, over my heart. "Can we change the subject? Why don't you try the dress on? Then we could go to a bar tonight or something."

She laughs. "Ivy, we're too young to get into a bar."

"We look way older than sixteen. You're telling me you haven't been into a bar? What? Ever?" Now I know what I can do for Callie. She totally needs to get out more—her mom was always too controlling. I say, "We're going to have so much fun."

"I don't know," she protests weakly. She starts folding a towel she's picked up from the floor.

"It's summer vacation. You deserve this. Tell you what, I'm going to be your ticket to the best summer ever. Like it was supposed to be last time." I pull off my dress and chuck it onto the floor.

"Okay, um . . ." She looks away.

Yep, she totally needs to loosen up. "Are you *blushing*?" I ask.

"Course."

"You've seen it all before."

"We're not kids now."

I shimmy across the room.

"Ivy!"

I giggle. "What?"

Callie smiles. "Nothing. Put some clothes on."

"If you let me paint your nails. And if you promise to wear my silver dress—"

Her phone rings and cuts me off.

Callie

Mom's calling. Whoops, I forgot to text her and I've been at Ivy's house for ages.

She says, "I'm on my way home now." Her voice is tight.

"What's wrong?"

"Your granny fell off that dreadful step. I knew she would. The hospital called."

"Hospital?"

"Your dad's tied up, just for an hour. I need you to watch Cosmo—please, love."

"Is Granny all right?"

Ivy pats a spot next to her on the bed and says softly, "You okay?"

Mom says, "Where are you? Aren't you at home? Is that Rebecca?"

"I'll be there in two minutes, don't worry. How's Granny?"

"She's all right. I think. Shaken. Look, I'll meet
you at home right away." Mom ends the call.

I sit next to Ivy, heavy suddenly. "My granny fell."

"Is she okay?"

"I think so. But I have to go. I have to babysit
Cosmo. I've never done that before."

"A baby can't be that hard to figure out. I'll come
help."

"Um, I think Mom would prefer it if I . . ."

Ivy shuffles closer. "I understand. Family."

I lean in to hug Ivy goodbye but she's doing that
European kissing thing. On the bed, we semi-hug
but Ivy ends up kissing my hair. Awkward.

Then I'm out of there. I hurry down the back
alleyway, the dust of summer on my sandalled feet,
the dirt of the day grimy on my clothes and hair,
the silky silver dress clutched in my hand.

The morning after Ivy walked back into my life, I'm
awake early. Not that I really slept for worrying
about Granny. I keep reminding myself that she
was released from the hospital, so it can't be too

bad, and that Mom and I are going to see her after breakfast. A warm breeze drifts through my open window, lifting the curtain, as if the day is peeping in. The sky is already bright although it's not even seven. I love the light in Edenville.

A line floats into my head. *She asked you to stop by the river when the world cracked open like an egg.* This happens to me all the time: words drift like bubbles in my mind, but I never write them down. I guess I feel like they'll look different, stupid somehow, if I do. At least I can write stuff for *Flat Earth Theory*; non-fiction feels more straightforward, as if there's a right way to do it. Mom's always eager when I write for the zine, overexcited, over-proud. I know, poor me! I should be pleased she's so interested in my writing but instead it makes me feel pressured to write something amazing, which makes my imagination curl up and die. A voice floats up outside my open window.

"Wake up, sleepyhead. Wake up, wake up."

I sit up and lean out the window. Ivy's standing on the grassy median in the middle of our street. She's wearing tight black shorts and an equally tight white workout top. No one else I know could make that look good. She's jogging on the spot, waving up at me.

"Come on, Callie."

"What are you doing awake so early?"

She yells, "Our first project is to get the weight off."

I may not have Ivy's fashion-model body, but still. "Um, no thanks."

"Not you! Me! Paranoid much? But I need a jogging partner." She keeps jogging lightly, moving from foot to foot as if the ground is too hot.

"You're already skinny."

She spins and taps her slender butt. "Gotta keep it up. My thighs are *huge*!" She jogs in a little circle, then another, looking up at me after each one and smiling.

"You don't need to lose weight, Ivy! Anyway, I'm not even out of bed."

"I won't take no for an answer. Come on." She starts doing jumping jacks.

"Oh my God! The whole world will see."

"Get up! Like now, or I'll have to serenade you."

I laugh. The breeze is fragrant with our neighbour's roses, and some sort of happy-vibe hits me. "Okay. Why not? Give me ten minutes. Only, don't sing!"

She sings, *"When the saints go marching in . . ."* One thing Ivy has never been able to do is carry a tune.

I duck away from the window and get out of bed. I don't think I have any clothes that'll remotely work for jogging, but Mom has one outfit for Zumba. I pad into her room to sneak it out of the drawer. She's not in bed. I expect she's tucked up with Cosmo in his room, which is painted with glorious, colourful fish. I hope she slept better than me, but I doubt it. Cosmo doesn't exactly sleep. I slip out of my PJs, squeeze into Mom's top and tug on the sweatpants.

I look at my parents' unmade bed. I don't have to wonder where Dad is. He works random hours to fit around Cosmo and Mom. I never know when he'll be home from the university. Looks like his day started even earlier than mine. I check my phone. I'll easily be back in time to go see Granny.

I slip on socks and my old sneakers. I look ridiculous.

Ivy sings loudly, *"All things bright and beautiful, / All creatures great and small, / All things wise and wonderful,* / *GO JOGGING IN THE MORNING!*"

I have to go before she wakes Cosmo.

The first part of the jog is absolute torture. Within twenty paces I feel like my lungs might catch fire. I can't get my breath. I try to keep up with Ivy, who's bounding ahead like a graceful deer, the soft light making her look like the lead in a Hollywood movie, and making me feel like the overworked camera-dude who carries the heavy equipment. I slow down, but Ivy doesn't seem to notice, so I force my aching legs to keep going. I check my phone, which has been bouncing around awkwardly in my pant pocket. We've been running for only four minutes and I'm going to die. Even when I go slower, the burning in my lungs gets worse and I feel a stabbing stitch.

"Ivy, stop," I gasp.

She skips back and grabs my arm so I can't collapse in a heap. She urges, "You've got to push past it. Keep running. At least keep walking. Trust me. Come on, we haven't even started."

She times us as we walk for two minutes, and then she encourages me to start jogging again. We go a little slower. This time, my lungs are okay, and although I'm really sweating I feel a bit more like I can handle it.

We alternate between walking and running, turning along streets I have never paid attention to, passing pretty clapboard houses I hardly remember seeing before. I feel like Odysseus travelling to exotic lands, and I wonder where the Lotus-Eaters are, or where the Cyclops lives. I'm a nerd.

Ivy interrupts my thoughts. "You're doing really well."

"My legs feel like jelly. How long do we run for?"

"Another minute, then we'll walk. Think you can handle it?"

"I had no idea I was so out of shape. This is killing me. You okay?"

She shrugs one shoulder. It's a gesture I remember perfectly. "Course. You're not much competition." She shoves me lightly.

"Yet. Give me a little time."

Now she's sailing ahead. "Just a bit longer. Nearly there. Nearly. Okay— NOW."

She slows and I stop, bending over at the waist to suck in air.

"Start walking. It'll feel better."

I lift my head and obey. We're in a neighbourhood that's not far from my house, but because I'm normally in the car, speeding through, I've never really paid attention to the different coloured doors, the small mailbox decorated with boats, the tiny white dog who barks at us with surprising ferocity, the meticulous garden with its froth of lilies. It must be the endorphins, or whatever, because suddenly I'm high.

That's when I see Kurt Hartnett coming out of an untidy yellow house, broken toys scattered in the front yard, a garbage bag lying unattended by the front door, one of the windows boarded up, the other semi-covered with what might be a pillowcase. He picks up the garbage bag, not noticing me; I'm glad because I'm a sweaty mess, my hair sticking up and yesterday's mascara (mascara being the only makeup I ever wear) probably streaked down my face. I wonder why he's here because Kurt doesn't live close to me; he lives on a big fancy acreage just outside town.

Ivy nudges me in the ribs with her elbow. "He's, like, cute."

"You think so?"

Kurt is broad shouldered, fairly tall, with cropped hair and almost-black eyes. Rebecca doesn't think he's cute, not rugged enough for her. Tilly thinks he's okay. I like the way he heads an editorial meeting, tapping his pen on the desk while waiting for us all to settle, then listening when someone has an idea, even if it sounds like a stupid one at first. I don't know if I find him cute, though. I just think he's cool. Today, he's wearing a blue T-shirt, short sleeves rolled up, showing off his biceps, and I spot a tattoo. As we get closer, I see it's Greek lettering: γνῶθι σεαυτόν. I wonder what it means. His muscles tighten as he heaves the garbage bag into a Dumpster.

He sees us. We're right near him on an empty street at really too-early o'clock. Also one of us is stunning and dressed in tight running clothes, her blonde hair luminous.

Kurt wipes his hands on his jeans and says, "You two look, yeah, energetic." He adds, "Hey, did you email me the piece yet?" His voice is soft and deep, like the low notes of a cello.

I say, "I'm going over it one last time."

"Perfectionist."

Ivy nudges me, then fills the silence I'm creating. "You two"—she waves a hand in my direction—"know each other? Come on, introduce me!" She flicks her hair with one long, tanned finger, the nail obscenely pink. The way she's looking at him, peering up through her eyelashes, it's like he's the only guy in the universe. He doesn't stand a chance.

"This is Kurt Hartnett. He goes to Edenville High. Year above us."

Ivy says, "I'm new around here."

"I guess so," he says, arching an eyebrow.

"So, what are the most fun things to do in town?" says Ivy.

"Depends what you find fun."

"Good music, parties, the usual." Ivy's phone beeps. She untucks her phone from her bra and checks it.

Kurt says to me, "I'll send you a couple edits on the scholarship article. I've got stuff to do, so we can't meet later." He glances at the rundown house, the tatty front yard. Then he says, "The board's discussing it first week of August, even though it's summer. You just know those douchebags—They'll pass it while everyone's looking the other way."

"I knew that piece wasn't quite ready. I should have waited to send it to you."

"It's great. Minor edits, that's all."

I wrote the piece on a wave of outrage. The scholarship program at our school gives a bursary to a kid who can't afford to go on to university, someone who shows merit. Many of the students who've received it in the past have gone on to run their own businesses, work in government, teach; one of them even became a brain surgeon. The school wants to cut it because of "funding difficulties."

I say, "First week of August?" I check my phone for the dates. "I'll make sure I'm there. Do a follow-up."

Ivy looks up from her phone and cries, "What piece? What are you guys even talking about?"

"Nothing. Come on, let's go," I say.

"It isn't nothing. It's big," Kurt says. He turns to Ivy. "It's an article for *Flat Earth Theory*."

Ivy laughs. "Now I'm really confused."

I say, "I'll tell you later."

"Hey, we're going down to the lake tomorrow," says Kurt. "My friend Xander and I are taking my boat out. We could pick you up."

"You have a boat?" Ivy asks. She casts a puzzled eye over the house.

Kurt tenses, ever so slightly, but I'm not sure Ivy registers. He says, "Yeah. My dad grew up sailing. So, wanna come?"

I'm about to tell him that we can't because my mom would never let me, no way, but Ivy speaks first and tells Kurt we'd totally love to. Then she gets his number, touches him lightly on the arm, tugs at me and starts jogging in a casual sexy way, looking as if she's completely at ease. Which I guess she is. I follow, then glance back at Kurt, who's shielding his eyes against the sun and watching us leave.

I call out, "Bye then."

Ivy jogs back in my direction. "Come on," she says.

Kurt nods slightly and goes into the house. I almost lose my footing on a rogue piece of sidewalk, and I twist around, flailing my arms and catching hold of Ivy before I fall.

She laughs and holds me up. "You okay?" She hugs me. "He's, like, delicious. I love the subtle type. He's so going to help me get over everything. You're the best."

When I get home, Mom's standing in the kitchen, bleary eyed, with flushed cheeks. Cosmo is in his sling hanging off her like a bald koala, nuzzling gummy-mouthed into her shoulder, and the first thing she says is, "You should have left a note."

My earlier buzz of pleasure is replaced by post-jog irritation. I say, "I didn't think you'd notice I'd gone."

Mom stops slicing the bread and deliberately puts down the knife. "Callie, stop." It's code for me to backtrack and gives me an easy out, but I'm not in the mood for an easy out. She adds, "I need to know where you are."

"I'm not a preschooler."

Cosmo must sense the tension. He squirms, then yells out, getting red in the face and arching his back, struggling within the soft material of the sling. I look at him, wondering, as I've wondered before, how it's possible that this tiny, grouchy, colicky creature could be related to me. It's hard to imagine myself as a baby like this, although the photos show I looked almost exactly like him at three months old.

Mom tickles Cosmo under the chin. Abruptly he stops crying and smiles. The emotions of a baby are so changeable. It seems to me that perhaps Cosmo and I have more in common than I'd thought, because I'm suddenly not irritated, just tired.

"I went jogging. I know, not like me." I smile, inviting conversation. "Sorry. I don't mean to be so grumpy."

Mom's not listening. Cosmo is all big open-mouthed smiles as she tickles. "Who's a happy baby now?" she says, casting me an apologetic look. "Hurry up and get ready, Callie."

I trudge toward the shower, worried again about Granny.

Mom has to let herself into Granny's with her key. Normally Granny opens her door all smiles. I feel a shudder of apprehension, especially as we walk through the empty sitting room and find Granny in her bed, sleeping. When I lean in to kiss her papery cheek, she smells of roses, as always, but also of sweat and something else. I don't even want to figure out that smell. I sit on the edge of her bed and clasp her petal-soft hand.

She stirs to say, "My goodness, I didn't know I was having company — now whatever do you think of me? No tea prepared, not even dressed." Despite the fact she moved to Edenville nearly seventy years ago, her British accent is strong. I sometimes hear myself dropping in a British word or phrase and I know it's her voice speaking through me. She struggles to sit, letting go of my hand.

I say, "Granny . . . ?" I choke up. "Sorry, I just . . ."

She settles into the cushions as I plump them around her head. "Callie, now then, I'm perfectly fine." She directs her next comment at my mother. "Goodness, Lizzy, I'm not an invalid. You didn't tell me Callie was coming with you today."

I know, because I know Granny so well, that she's furious. She doesn't want me seeing her in bed like this. There's a little tug at my heart as if someone is putting in a stitch. "Sorry, Granny. I wanted to visit. Dad's looking after Cosmo and I thought it'd be a good time."

"Of course." She lifts one spider-veined hand and says, "Elizabeth, should we have tea?"

Obediently Mom slips out of the room to the kitchen.

I call after her, "I can get it, Mom."

Granny says to me brightly, "No, no, you sit with me."

"How are you feeling?"

"Now, now, girl. I'm not off my perch yet." Her hands follow my gaze and immediately begin to tidy loose strands of her hair, pinning them up. She emerges as her usual self from the frail bed-bound creature and lowers her voice to say, "So, what's my favourite granddaughter been doing?"

"Your *only* granddaughter."

"Exactly."

"Not much. Hanging out. How are you feeling?"

"It was Madeline who was the problem." Her eyes have softened. She says, "Not easy to forgive. Now, Joanie, have you ever seen anything like it?"

"Granny," I say, "it's me, Callie."

"Ah, yes. Now, dear, silly me. And you are?"

That stitch becomes a row of stitches.

She says, "Oh, it was fun when I was young—When I came here, dear, there was nothing, really. I thought the outhouses were little sheds—outdoor toilets! Goodness, what a thing. I wrote telling them I lived like a queen, but it wasn't true."

I wait, listening. After the pause becomes too long, I say, "Did you miss home?"

"It wasn't like today. It was like crossing into a . . . Oh, it was a different world then." Her eyes brighten. "Callie, dear. It's so good to see you! We must have tea."

"Mom's making some."

"Is she? Marvellous. What's new with you?"

I've never seen her like this and I struggle to make conversation. "Um. You remember my friend Ivy?"

"Ivy . . . The one with the *mother*?" Suddenly she's as sharp as scissors.

"Please, don't bring that up."

"Of course not."

"So, um, Ivy's back. We went jogging this morning."

"That sounds fun."

"I just wish I was . . . as confident as her. She

met this friend of mine today and he blatantly likes
her. She's stunning."

"Oh, Callie, my love. So are you."

"That's what they pay you to say."

She laughs, completely back to her normal,
gossipy, interested self. "I wish I'd known how
beautiful I was when I was younger. It all fades,
my darling. Now, is there going to be trouble
with Ivy's mother? Should you talk to your mom?
Should I?"

"Let me see first, okay?"

Her eyes get misty. "I always wished I'd run
away with the circus. Bet you didn't know your
old granny could juggle."

Mom comes back into the room with a tray
set with three china cups, a china vase and three
chocolate biscuits. She glances over, frowning
slightly. "What are you two whispering about?"

Granny says, "I'd love to walk the tightrope, just
once. I'll never do that now, will I."

Mom is quiet as she pours the tea.

✳

We leave Granny's for the short walk home. The air is scented and birds are singing. It's much easier to think about other things than about Granny. Thinking about Granny makes me feel unmoored, scared. Instead, I float in la-la land. Somehow, magically, Mom will let me go on the boat with Ivy, *tra la la*.

"Mom, so, um, I was, um, wondering if I could go out on my friend's boat tomorrow. After visiting Granny. We don't have anything going on, do we?"

But she's not that sort of parent. Her mom-radar is always switched on and now it's flashing red.

"What boat?" she says.

"It's no big deal. He's just this guy from school. He asked me to go on his boat tomorrow with another friend."

"Who is he?"

"He's the editor guy. I've told you about him. Kurt Hartnett."

"No, you haven't."

"I *have*. It'll be fine. He's nice." Most people my age wouldn't even have to ask their mom permission, but my family doesn't work like that. My mom is all about keeping children children for as long as possible. Her books are described as *charming, innocent, whimsical.*

"We should go and see your grandmother again tomorrow."

"I know. I said *after* that. Please, Mom, you have to let me go."

She sets her jaw firmly. I know what that means. It means she's veering toward no.

I say, "It's not just him. Ivy will be there."

She actually stops walking. "Ivy? Ivy who? What? Ivy Foulds?"

I nod.

"She's *here*?"

"She got back yesterday. I was at her house when you called about Granny."

"Her house? Ivy Foulds? My love, I don't think this is a good idea."

"Are you really going to do this again?"

"You were devastated when she left."

"That wasn't her fault!"

Mom asks, "Were you with Ivy when you went jogging?"

"Jogging's good for me. It's not like I was doing something dangerous!"

Her face pinches. She starts to walk again, so I walk too. She says, "I don't want to fight with you. I'm exhausted, I'm worried about your granny, and now this."

I say, quietly, "Please, Mom. I just want to go on a boat with some friends."

"You've always been intoxicated with that girl. Think about it—remember how you treated poor Rebecca?"

"We were just kids—what does it even matter now?"

We're back at the house. Mom opens the door and says, "Your friendship with Ivy wasn't good for you three years ago, why do you think it would be now?"

"I know what this is about—"

"This is about surrounding yourself with good people, like Rebecca."

We're standing in the corridor. Dad looks at us from his spot on the couch, bemused. Cosmo lies on his front on a blanket on the living room floor, cooing.

I'm *never* like this, but thoughts of Ivy going on the boat with Kurt, flicking her hair about, letting her tanned hand slide into his—these thoughts sting like little wasps. I say more loudly than I intend, "I've had enough of this, enough of feeling like—"

Cosmo's face crumples.

Mom says, "Now look what you've done. Callie, we all keep pretending that you're *not* being utterly selfish. Do you comprehend how tired I am? How much I'd like a little help?"

"I didn't ask for you guys to have a baby! Everything's always Cosmo, Cosmo, Cosmo."

Mom slams her hand on the hallway table. "How dare you talk to me like this? You are not to see her. Do you understand?"

"What are you talking about?"

"You cannot see Ivy. That's it." Her cheeks are red. Cosmo starts really screaming.

"I'm sixteen."

"Until I see you acting like an adult, I'm going to treat you like a child. You are forbidden from seeing her."

Forbidden? I'm out of there. I storm upstairs and slam the door. It doesn't make me feel better. I sob

into the pillow like a girl in a love story, then text Ivy to tell her I can't make it for the boat trip.

She calls immediately. "Callie, what's going on? Is your granny okay?"

I'm embarrassed to hear the words catch in my throat. "Sorry. I just had a fight with Mom."

"I'll come over."

"She's not exactly gonna let me have friends over right now. And there's no way I can come tomorrow."

She doesn't even pause. "On the boat? No problem. We'll just tell Kurt that we'll go another day."

My heart lifts. I look out the window at the lush leafy trees and bright skies beyond. I say, "That would be cool." I get up and start to straighten my desk, wiping the surface down with a Kleenex.

"I'd feel lonesome without you there, anyways."

"God, I hate fighting with her."

"I know how *that* feels. You okay?"

"I just . . . I dunno. Mom's all worried about Granny. Granny wasn't really herself—she was dreamy, forgetful. I thought falling from the step wasn't a big deal but she seems to have hit her

head pretty hard. I probably should've been nicer to Mom."

"This sucks. Maybe if I ask your mom to let you come?"

Um, huge problem there. But I can't tell Ivy I've been banned from seeing her. It's too insane. I say, "No. I'm being unfair. You should go on the boat. You're new here and settling in."

"Really? Only if you're okay with it."

"Course."

"Are you sure, sure?"

"Absolutely. Tell me how it goes, 'kay?" I lie back on the bed. Pity party number ten thousand. Sometimes, I'm my own worst enemy.

THREE

JULY 31ST

Kurt

We arrive at the hospital. Hustle into the ER. There's a bored woman at Information, checking her phone. Xander asks questions. The woman's mouth thins. I hear her say, "If you're not family, there's nothing we can do. You have to wait."

I say, "Can't you tell us anything?"

She doesn't even answer.

Xander walks away. I follow. A long, grey hallway,

doors open all the way along, ill-looking people inside. Stench of bleach, bad food, misery. Now we're in a small space with three leather couches. A TV show-ing cartoons. A woman crouched over.

I mutter to Xander, "That must be Ivy's mom."

She looks like Ivy, but less natural — over-yellow hair, Botox-fixed skin. At first, she doesn't turn to us. Instead, her jaw hangs slack, her bottom row of white teeth exposed. The buttons are done up wrong on her silky cream shirt. She stands and looks straight at me, her eyes blank as two pebbles.

"Mrs. Foulds?" Xander says.

Her gaze shifts. She has one hand pressed to her chest. Trying to stop her heart from blasting out of there and exploding in our faces. She says, "They don't know much. It's bad. I'm just waiting, they told me to wait. Not here. Somewhere else. But I can't. I can't wait there. Not with the other parents —"

I want to ask about Callie, but Mrs. Foulds is bab-bling. "The doctor said wait here. It's quieter. My Kevin's away for the night — he has to travel all the time, even just after we got back to Edenville . . . trips . . . he's very important — He's on his way though, soon. He'll find me. The doctors will find me —"

Xander cuts her off gently, like he's talking to a child, shakes her hand. "I'm Xander Buckmaster. I'm a friend of Ivy. And Kurt. Would you like a cup of coffee?"

Man, Xander is brilliant. So calm.

Mrs. Foulds nods. She grips Xander's arm. "My baby. I know I've made mistakes but I . . . I may not be a perfect mother but I love my daughter."

"Of course," says Xander. Calm. Calm.

Mrs. Foulds says, "She's going to be okay. She has to be."

But none of us are going to be okay. Ever again.

TWELVE DAYS EARLIER

Ivy

Kurt beeps the horn outside my house. Mom's asleep on the couch. She's gorgeous when she's sleeping. I spot a text on her phone from Kevin. Dirty words. Gross. I tuck the phone next to her. She stirs, the sour stink of her rising like steam. Screw it, Mom, two days we've been back. Don't you think Kevin's gonna notice? I take the bottle.

The room is dark, curtains drawn. No one's watching but I check around anyway. I put the bottle to my lips and hold it there. Then, slowly, I take the bottle away from my mouth. I *won't* drink. I'm *not* like her—*see how easy it is, Mom, not to drink?* We're the result of the choices we make every day and this is my choice. I pour the bottle out into the sink, wishing she didn't always find a way to get more. But I'm not going to waste energy thinking like that. I count *one, two, three, four, five.*

I'm ready for the boat trip. Summery dress for a sunny, summery day. Kurt beeps the horn again. I've made him wait long enough, poor boy. Men are like dogs, they need training, and every dog needs a reward when he's done good. Kurt has been very patient. I pop gum in my mouth, step down the porch stairs and slide into the back because there's another guy in the passenger seat—a thin guy with a beard and glasses, crouched over because he's so tall. He swivels to face me.

"Hi," I say to him, "I'm Ivy."

He nods a hello. "Xander." I'm guessing he's every-one's friend—the one who fixes stuff if it's broken.

"Callie can't make it," I say. I'm bummed she's not coming, leaving me on my own with two cute guys. Nothing I haven't handled before, of course, but it would be a million times more fun with her. I ask Kurt, "Can I smoke in here?"

He shakes his head. "My dad's car."

"I should probably quit anyways." I *love* to smoke. Love everything about it, especially that first, fabulous drag. But as the words are coming out of my mouth, I realize it's true. It might be time to quit. New town, new life.

Xander asks, "Where you from, Ivy?"

Kurt starts the car. He looks like Diego from this angle. My heart sputters. I don't know how I didn't see it when we met, but sitting here, Kurt could *be* Diego. A better Diego, softer features, fuller mouth. I say, "I was living in Kansas City for about a year. Then a tornado brought me here—just like Dorothy."

"So this is Oz?" Kurt asks.

I say, "Without the wicked witch."

"And you like it?"

"I lived here three years ago but just for the summer. Before that, I lived in Paris, Lille, New York, Madison, Calgary, Fort McMurray, uh, a few other places. I like it here as much as anywhere."

Kurt says, "How come so many moves?"

Mom says the best way to talk to men is to let them do the talking. Stay mysterious. She may not be the best mother in the world, but she sure seems to be able to find boyfriends. "Enough about me," I say. "Tell me about this boat."

Callie

Mom's working, Cosmo hanging from her in his sling, the keys tap, tap, tapping away. I imagine her usual bad music playing in her headphones. I watch her for a second. When I was little, I used to play on her office floor, waiting for her to finish an illustration. We used to look at her work together, long before she started publishing and sharing it with everyone else. I hover by the office door. I should just ask her if I can go see Ivy, who must be home from the boat trip by now. Mom pulls out one ear of her headphones.

"What, Callie?"

Her tone doesn't encourage me. I say, "Nothing."

I return to my bedroom and text Ivy: **Whatcha doing?**

We arrange to meet up in a café that didn't exist three years ago called Mystical Java. I can't believe I'm going to do this. I peek out of my room. Mom's on the phone—blah, blah, some problem with her artwork, the design's too busy and needs streamlining, something. I tiptoe past her office, sneaking down the stairs. Just like that, I'm out the front door. Cosmo starts yelling with perfect timing. I let out a tight breath, my heart boom-bumpity in the breezy sunshine.

I cross the street under the overhang of leaves that arch from huge, old trees. A cat startles and yowls, scurrying for cover as I head past the first couple of stores that begin yuppified Pine Hill Street, which is full of cafés, bars, restaurants, yoga studios and expensive clothing stores. I pass the cupcake counter of Cakes for Two, and open the door of Mystical Java to the smell of roasting coffee and fresh baked goods. It's full of people typing on laptops or chatting on their phones. The

lineup is too long for me to join right away, so, as
I'm early, I decide to wait for Ivy before ordering
coffee. I sit at the magically free table by the window and drum my fingers.

I catch sight of a flyer pinned to the wall.
Underneath the word *ARTSTARTS*, brightly
coloured doodles surround the smiling face of a
preschooler. The flyer reads: *Assistant Wanted for
Art Classes for Kids*. I wonder if I could do that. I
do need a job. I key the number into my cell, but
I don't call. Instead, I check my email, check the
time, watch a couple of videos my friends have
posted.

If I were Ivy, I'd call right away. So I do it.

A woman answers, "Ana Stevens. Artstarts."
Kids yell in the background.

My hands get clammy. "I'm calling about the job."

"That's great. Hold on. I can't hear anything
in here." I imagine she's put her hand over the
receiver, because her voice is muffled as she says to
someone else, "I'll just head out for a sec, okay?" A
door bangs shut. It gets quieter. Ana says, "So, we
run a program at the gallery over the summer and
it's very popular. Our student helper quit on me

and I, well, I hate to say it, but I desperately need someone to provide another pair of hands. Crowd control." She laughs.

"Sure. So you're at the gallery?"

"That's right."

"I love the gallery."

"Okay, tell me more about you."

"My name's Callie Carraway. Um, I start Grade Eleven in September and art is one of my subjects. And, I like little kids." At least, I *think* I do. Although, as I say it I realize I never really do anything with Cosmo, but then again, he's a *baby*. Little kids are way more fun, always asking questions and stuff.

Ana says, "Could you swing by tomorrow? Ten in the morning? For an informal interview. I'll tell you what we pay, and we'll get to know each other. If it goes well, we might have you start right away. To be honest, we pretty much need someone, well, ASAP."

"Okay, sure, great," I say.

As I get off the phone with Ana, Ivy bursts into the café. That's the right word for it. She bursts in, the door swinging shut behind her, and

I swear there's a slight pause in the conversations, a moment when the other customers assess her, the men taking a longer look than necessary, the women feeling slightly less comfortable than they did before. I wonder what it would be like to have that effect on the world, to always have people look at you and size you up, to have jealousy and desire fluttering around you like small dark shadows.

Ivy smiles, her white teeth emphasized by a hot pink lipstick that matches her bright nails. Oblivious to people watching her, she calls across the café, "What do you want? My treat. I'll get us Green Tea Lattes. No, how about a Berry Burst Smoothie. That sounds healthy."

"I was gonna have coffee."

"Trust me — this is way more delicious and you'll feel better afterward."

The hot guy at the counter with the dreadlocks, the one who never even raises his gaze to me, fumbles her change.

Her perfume floats over like a fine mist as she joins me at the table. "So, how's your granny?"

"I dunno, frail."

Ivy says, "She's gonna be okay, though?"

"I hope so. It's not like her to be in bed in the day. She's always been on the go, cleaning up your cup before you've finished drinking your tea, chatting about adventures she plans, trips, ideas, wanting to learn how to text when my phone buzzes. She was a war bride—ran away from everyone she knew to come here. Her being in bed is like . . . like me table dancing in here."

"I'll get you table dancing." Ivy taps the back of my hand with her middle finger.

I say, "I like your ring."

"Diego gave it to me."

I follow her lead. "Who's Diego?"

Her eyes gleam. "Oh, Callie. There's so much you don't know."

I say, "I want to know about the boat trip. How was it?" Details, texture, moments that have now slipped away forever; I want them recreated by Ivy for me so I can feel the wind in her hair. Would Kurt have kissed her? Look at that pink mouth— of course he kissed her. Our drinks arrive, froufrou concoctions of yogourt and berries, cold, and admittedly good. I suck loads of mine down, thinking now about how we once spent an afternoon making smoothies in my kitchen. Ivy came up with the recipes and together we blended, tasted, giggled and invented ridiculous names for our drinks.

Ivy says, "I wish you'd been there. Xander's nice, but, uh, the *three* of us. Kinda weird. Kurt blatantly wanted it to be just us two, but there isn't much room on a small boat. Oooh, I have a great idea. You'd *love* Xander. Let's double date. Tonight. You and me, and them. God, Kurt's just my type, like Diego."

"'Kay. Tell me already. Who's Diego?"

"He was, like, my soulmate. Here's a pic." She gets her phone from her bra and shows me a blurry image of a guy looking over his shoulder at the camera. His black eyes smoulder and he's all poser-pouty. He wears a leather jacket and I think he's sitting on a motorbike. I reach for the phone but Ivy holds on to it. She says, "Cute, hey? Do you think he looks like Kurt?"

"Not really."

She considers the image. "I think he does."

"So, how long were you and Diego together?"

She slides her phone away. "Forget Diego. We

should live in the moment. Tonight sounds good, okay?"

"I don't know about double dating."

"It'll be great."

"Where are we going?" I don't know why I'm asking. There's no way Mom will let me go. I'm not even allowed to be at this café with Ivy. As I think this, I also know with sudden ferocity that I don't want to miss out. I don't want to lose Ivy again by always having to say no. I say, "Actually, don't tell me. It'll be easier to lie to Mom."

"Why lie?"

"It doesn't matter. Look, I'll sneak out. Somehow."

Ivy frowns.

I ask, "Have you got something good I can wear?"

I'm helpful around the house for the evening. I play with Cosmo, even changing his disgusting diaper. Mom and I aren't exactly speaking, but we're not shouting at each other either. She must assume that now she's laid down the rules, I'll simply follow. She didn't even notice that I went out earlier. She's so wrapped up with the new book, she thought I was in my room the whole time. She gets like this toward the end of a project. A bit fuzzy round the edges.

Dad's busy too. The university is on summer break, has been for a few weeks, but he's organized some conference on oral storytelling. Two smartly dressed women and two bearded men arrive at the house to talk about the influence of Greek epics on contemporary poetry. Together they burble off to the conference. Dad gets back around ten, singing quietly to himself, and thumps up the stairs to his office in the attic.

I lie in bed listening to the floorboards creak up there. Will he never go to sleep? I'm fully dressed under the covers. I've never sneaked out at night before. I've read books where characters do it, but—ridiculously—I've always been scared *they* might get caught, and never dared to do it myself.

I flick through the pages of *Bonjour Tristesse*, not really reading. With a sigh, I turn back to the beginning. The book is so short, I should have finished it already, but I can't concentrate at all. Lines spring out at me . . . *I have known boredom, regret, and occasionally remorse, but never sorrow . . . That summer,*

I was seventeen and perfectly happy . . . tall and almost beautiful, with the kind of good looks that immediately inspires one with confidence . . . Finally, finally I hear Dad's clumping feet on the wooden stairs from the attic to the main floor. The faucet, the buzz of his electric toothbrush, the flushing of the toilet, then the bedroom door closes. Cosmo cries out, but is soon quiet.

I make myself wait another twenty minutes. I push back the covers and line up a couple of pillows to make the bed look like I'm still in it—nerd that I am—then I open my window. A tree waits gracefully there, the branches inviting me, almost accusing me: *Why haven't you done this before, Callie?*

I haul myself out, scratching my hand on a sharp twig. I suck in a tiny cry of pain, wait until I'm sure I've woken no one, then pull myself easily into the tree. I twist around and lower the window so it's only open a crack, making sure I can lift it again later, then I clamber down the rough bark of the trunk, my heart racing, and pad onto the grass. The yard at night is softer, somehow, and yet spooky. Ghosts lurk here. There's a loud rustling by the garbage can and I almost have a heart attack. A cat slinks away. *Calm down, girl.* I don't even glance back at my house. I'm free.

I text Ivy: **On my way.**

She texts back: **Cool**, along with a picture of her wearing a short dress, one in her usual white. There are artful folds around the waist and neck. It offsets her tan and glittery gold makeup.

I get to Ivy's front door. Through the window, I see her mother watching TV in the lounge. She's thin and beautiful, wearing a flimsy pale shirt and jeans. She looks, I realize, like Ivy. I haven't seen her since that day three years ago, and now the memory is vivid. My skin prickles as I force it away, best forgotten; it has no impact on the present.

I knock gently. There's a pause, then Mrs. Foulds opens the door. A strange metallic sound buzzes around her. It's hard to place and it's only as her eyes widen in recognition that I realize the sound is coming from her phone. She's lifting it to her ear, not saying hello to me but to the person at the other end, and then, as she turns away, she slams the door in my face.

Thoughts burst in my head like bubbles, pop,

pop, pop. *She just slammed the door in my face. She smells of liquor. She makes me feel like I'm thirteen again.*

The door swings open again and Ivy appears. She swoops me into a hug and says, "Hi, gorgeous. I'm sooo glad you're here. So, we should, like, get ready."

I can sense in the way she rushes her speech, the way she shifts from one foot to the other, glancing over her shoulder, that she's nervous. Her mother has disappeared.

I say, "Um, everything okay? It's just—"

She cuts me off by waving a hand in the air and pulling me inside. Another thought pops in my head. *Ivy's mom hates me.* I'm suddenly queasy.

Up in her room, Ivy admires the effects of her make-over on me. She has pinned my black hair so it looks like I've cut it short, and my long bangs have tiny ringlets that hang seductively on one side of my face. She smudged deep pink along my cheekbones, eye-lids and lips, using the same pot for all three and then giving me the pot to keep. She put on two coats of mascara, which widens my eyes as if someone's told me a juicy secret. Her green silky shift and leggings are tight on me, but they still look good. We have the same size feet so I'm wearing her ankle boots. She's redone my nails in sparkly silver, nothing like my normal style — I mean, my normal non-style. I admire the girl looking at me from the glass. Who am I?

My phone buzzes on Ivy's bed. Rebecca texts me: **Home. Can't wait 2 c u early early early tmr!**

I text back: **Great xxx**. I tuck the phone into my bra, like Ivy does. It's the only place to put it.

Ivy reaches into her wardrobe and pulls out a silver flask. "It's Mom's. I, uh, borrowed it. Wanna drink?"

I shake my head, catching sight of myself in the mirror again. My cheekbones seem more structured in this light, like I have a face shape other than pudgy.

She says, "We're going out, we're allowed to have fun."

"Really, I'm fine."

She unscrews the lid and tips the flask to her lips. She swallows, pulls a face, wipes her mouth and sucks air through her lips. "Don't worry. I

shop like her but I don't drink like her. I only do it
for fun—like tonight." She holds out the flask. It's
engraved with swirly letters. "Vodka," she says.

"Does your Mom still . . .? I had no idea, really
none, when you lived here before."

"She hides it well. Practice, I guess. Look, can
we talk about something else? How about . . . how
about a drinking game. We could play Truth. You
know, it's like Truth or Dare but there are no dares.
Ask me anything. Drink for yes answers."

"I'm not sure—"

"It'll be fun. Look at you, you're gorgeous and
we're hanging out and everything's just as it should
be except you need to relax a little. Take a deep
breath. Tell you what, you go first. Ask me anything."

I'm tempted. There's so much I want to know.
"Okay. I guess so."

"Go on then."

I come out with "Okay. Since you left . . . did you
ever . . .? With a boy?"

She's already sipping from the flask as I ask and
she laughs so hard she sprays the air with vodka.
"You're so adorable and innocent. We have to be
careful you don't get eaten alive in the big wild

world. If you're talking about"—she lowers her voice dramatically—"sex . . ."

I blush. "It was a stupid question. You go first."

"Nooo, this is fun." She takes a long swig. "And yes, I have."

There's a huge silence, then I burst out laughing. "Ivy, that's the worst answer ever. You have to give me more than that."

"It's supposed to be yes or no! You want details?"

I blush harder, but I'm enjoying myself too.

She says, "First, your turn. Drink now if you want. Get it over with."

She passes me the flask, which is surprisingly cool to the touch, and heavy. I turn it from one side to the other, trying to decipher the writing, Latin, it seems. I quickly lift it to my lips and drink. I don't take one sip, but three, the burning taste hard to stomach, but it makes me want to prove myself more. I'm not the silly little girl I thought I was; it's time for me to grow up.

"Yeah, Callie," Ivy says approvingly. "My turn. Did you ever tell anyone?"

My tummy roils. I tell a sort of truth: "No."

"Really?"

"Really."

She grabs the flask. "Now, you wanted details. Well, it hurt, but not as much as I thought. I was fourteen. Mom was doing her thing, dating some guy. He lived in a craphole called Plato, so we lived there with him.

"Sooo, the sex. Gross. The guy Mom was dating, well, his son's name was Riley. He was arrogant, rat-faced, always wore a cap, two years older than me. Spent money quicker than his dad. He bought me a dress and we went up to the top bedroom. He wasn't a bad kisser, told me to peel the dress off, told me to spin around like I was some sort of porn star, watched me lie back . . . then we, you know. It took about two minutes."

A nasty little worm crawls under my skin.

She sips from the bottle and says, "Boy number two was great. Raunchy and fun. Number three was perfect, candles, the works. Number three . . . You have no idea." She says this with a funny expression on her face, like now she's an adult and I'm just a kid with no clue. But she's not mocking me, no, it seems that she's sad.

I say, "I feel like a loser."

"There's no rush, really. You should wait. I

should have waited. Okay, now you're warmed up." She giggles. "Who's your biggest crush?"

I drink several sips. The alcohol is warm in my throat. "I thought we were doing yes and no questions?"

"You changed the rules. So?"

It seems lame not to have an answer. I scrunch up my face as I try to think of someone. "Um, Kurt's friend. I mean, I don't know him well, but I've seen him hanging out with Kurt at school and I've always wanted to talk to him."

She squeals with delight. "Xander? I knew it. He's perfect. Quirky and sweet and smart. Like you."

I feel a little surge of pleasure. "Ego boost."

She says, "Pass that to me. Your question."

"Has your mom ever got any help?"

She screws the lid back on the flask.

"Come on, Ivy. You said I could ask anything."

"Let's just say, if anyone asks, it never happened. Okay?" Her eyes make her look like a baby rabbit that's been left out in the snow. She says more quietly, "I worry she'll do it again. You know?"

I want to say that I don't know, no, I *have no idea*.

The mood has shifted, grown melancholy. "I'm sorry," I say. "I didn't mean to spoil everything."

She manages a smile. "It's okay. The game was stupid anyway. We should go."

Night seeps over us as we walk arm in arm down the alley behind Ivy's house toward a bar I've passed a million times on my way to and from school with Rebecca. We'd always planned to go together one day, but instead I'm here with Ivy. I shake off the thought. Music pulses from within as we join the short queue below the large silver lettering of the sign that reads BEneath. I've burst out of my world into a whole new planet.

Ivy whispers, "What's your name?"

"You forgot me already?" I joke, before I realize she's passing me something. It's an ID card with a photo of a dark-haired girl who looks nothing like me. *Isabel Cabezas*.

Ivy has a secret smile, like she's just handed me the moon. ID. I hadn't even *thought* about it. I say, "I don't look like her."

"I know."

"Who is she? How come you have her card?" I study it. "Isabel Cabezas," I read. Born Kansas City. I recite her birthdate, making sure I get the year right.

The queue is moving forward and older people ahead are laughing, chatting, relaxed. I'm never going to get into this bar, I'm too young. There's no way.

"Trust me," says Ivy.

And in that moment, I do. I have a vivid memory of when we were thirteen: Ivy whispering, "Trust me."

The queue shuffles forward more and I don't even have time to be nervous as the bored security guy checks my ID, looks me over, nods slightly. He doesn't seem to realize the girl in the photograph is a completely different person. He waves me in. I step forward, the music wrapping itself around me, the vodka in my blood making my confidence soar.

BEneath is very full. There are lots of older people dancing, pressed together. Blue and white lights ghost over the moving bodies. We walk along the edge. The booths look more like beds, and people lie on them, listening to music, drinking, watching each other.

Kurt and Xander are standing by the bar. Words fall out of my mouth before I can stop them. "Wow, this place is amazing. I've never been here, no . . . I mean, it's not even two blocks from my house and I never even knew it was so cool."

"Callie, you need to sit down," Kurt says, leaning to talk into my ear. "Want some water?"

Ivy smiles and brushes by to say something to Kurt. I can smell her perfume. Her skin is silky. She catches my eye, indicating with a glance that this is a good time for me to talk to Xander. I nod and say, "Xander and I could, um, get drinks."

Xander seems to hear me and he mouths the word *Drinks*.

We walk away from Kurt and Ivy. Their absence is like a cool liquid seeping through my dress. A line pops into my head: *The space you never filled, a water glass spilled.*

I glance back. They're huddled together. Ivy shrugs one shoulder. God, I'd love to be like that, so provocative yet comfortable, so sexy. Maybe I *could* be like that. In the heat of bodies around me, squeezing between the sweaty dancers, I realize I'm drunk. I'm dizzy, delirious drunk. I take a

couple of dance steps, leaving Xander to get the
bartender's attention, and move closer to Ivy, who
stops talking to Kurt and starts dancing.

I hear myself laugh. "This is fun, Ivy!" I yell.

She cups my ear and yells back. "We're only just
getting started!"

FOUR

JULY 31ST

Kurt

Xander checks his phone. Looks down the hospital hallway. Stares at the floor. Mrs. Foulds perches on the couch. The lamp on the small table flickers, a single blinking eye. With the old couches and the cartoons blabbing on the TV, the waiting area looks like my birth-mom's living room. I remember when I was no bigger than that TV. Eating fries. Dipping them in ketchup. The rug had a hole in it. I stuck my finger through.

Mom lay next to me, half asleep, giggly. I loved her most like that. I stroked her black hair. She pushed me off, growling, "Don't get ketchup on me." Then there was that knock on the door.

My head hurts. I sit on the other couch. Look around. Touch the dollar around my neck. Rest my chin on my hands, which are pointed upright as if I'm praying. I'm not religious, don't go to church or anything, but deep down I know someone's there. There's gotta be. Xander with-draws and pads off down the hallway. I'm left with Mrs. Foulds. The hum of the hospital is my soundtrack. I need a cigarette. Or a pen. Something in my hands.

Can't help wondering about the last few min-utes in the car and how they ended up going off the bridge. Did they know what was coming? Or was it stomach-lurching-through-the-eyeballs shock, like on a roller coaster.

This is sick.

A doctor approaches. White-haired, odd eyes — each a different colour. He says, "Mrs. Foulds, come with me, please."

She nods, raising one hand to her mouth.

He gives nothing away. The sound of their shoes echoes down the hallway as they retreat.

This is what it means to be alone.

TWELVE DAYS EARLIER

Ivy

Callie's shiny-eyed drunk. I shake it on the dance floor with her, then dance over to Kurt, who says something I can't hear. His cheek stubbly, his mouth close to my ear, the sound sharp in my eardrums. I dance super close, and he moves with me. My boobs squish against him, sorta accidental. Guys like that; it makes them feel like a protector. Mom always goes on about how men need to be the saviour, or something like that. Seems to me like guys just want to get laid. Christ, Kurt looks like Diego. With my eyes half closed, I could be back in Diego's arms. Now I'm nearly crying. Lame.

Kurt points to Callie dancing with Xander. Kurt seems to be saying he wants us to head over. I look up at him through my lashes. A major Mom trick.

The tip of my tongue flickers out of the corner of my mouth. Diego couldn't resist but Kurt has a faraway expression, as if he's not in the room at all. It makes me *really* want him.

I put my index finger on his cheek and he stops staring off into space. I beckon him to follow. There's a lineup near the washrooms and I lead him past it, along a hallway until we find a quieter room full of couches and beds, hanging fabrics, trippy music. I pull him down next to me so we're half sitting and half leaning on each other on a huge cushion.

I say, "I'm not usually this, uh, forward."

He raises an eyebrow. "No?"

"Don't tease." I laugh and pick imaginary fluff from the cushion. "So, what's the deal with the house?"

"What?"

"You've got a boat like that and then you're taking out the trash at that place."

"It's nothing."

"'Fess up."

He scratches the back of his head. I wait—people don't like silence, they want to fill it. He says, "My birth-mom. I visit her sometimes, help out."

I wait for him to say more and he does, lowering his voice. "I don't like talking about her. Everyone knows anyways. Edenville's not exactly . . . She's not, yeah . . . it's kind of . . ." A muscle pulses in his neck.

I say, "I didn't mean to dig . . ."

"I was adopted when I was five."

"Right."

"My adopted mom met me through her work at a shelter, fell in love. Later they had Sam, then Adrian. Naturally. Not adopted, I mean. It's all pretty sweet. Dad runs the brewery here—big house. Boat. Most people think my life's sugar-coated. Like Callie's. And her perfect family. Can't imagine any different."

"You and her?" I leave a pause.

"No." He scratches the back of his head again, checks his phone.

I say, "Not everyone knows—people like Callie live in one world and we live in the other."

He puts his phone in his pocket. "Yeah, something like that. Except I don't live there anymore."

"That's the sort of thinking I admire," I say. The huge cushion has tipped us pretty close. It's easy for me to lift my mouth and kiss him quickly on the lips. He leans back, surprised, and considers. There we go. I kiss him again. Good kisser. Sweet.

His hand moves to my waist. I slide it lower but then I'm first to pull away. Always leave them wanting more. Kurt looks like he's surfacing. He has a lazy smile.

We get up to go dance. Closer now, sweaty, hands laced.

Callie comes back to my house. She's one of those fun, giggly drunks. I'm the moody type and I'm coming down from the high of kissing Kurt. She chats about a sleepover we had three years ago when we mixed up face cream with hair remover and waited for ages for the hair on our legs to dissolve, but it never did. She laughs all over again at the idea of putting hair remover on our faces.

I shove her onto the bed.

Callie says, "Not that we have hair on our faces!"

"True."

"Ivy?"

"Yeah?"

"Can I ask another question?"

"I'm sorta tired."

"What was it like, kissing Kurt?"

I know I'm going to want to go over every detail with Callie in the morning, but right now I just want to sleep this off, so I shrug. "Pretty nice. Callie, let's get some sleep. Want water?"

She tucks herself around a pillow. "I'm glad you're home."

Man, she's so sweet. Like mosquito bites, tears prick my eyes. Callie puffs the pillow behind her head, lies back, and passes out, snoring softly. Fast asleep. I snuggle up to her. Being here next to her makes me remember. I don't want to think about it, but the memory comes hard.

The last day we lived in Edenville, three years ago, Callie and I went for a walk by the river. We glimpsed a woman standing at the edge of the riverbank far below, her bare feet in the dirt. She was teetering at the edge, her arms spread. My fucking mother.

Callie cried, "Oh my God, Ivy."

"Just shut up." I became still. Small. Listening.

"What's she doing?"

I said, "No, no, no."

Mom raises her arms, reaching toward the rushing river. We scramble down the slope. I scream, "Mom, it's me!"

The woman half turns to us, her mouth a round O of surprise. I lose my footing, and Callie tumbles through the shrubs, yelling. She manages to get close enough to grab Mom's dress strap.

Mom flinches and snarls at her, "It's your fault. My own daughter would rather be with you than with me."

I yell, "No!"

Mom hears me, looks over at me, then jumps.

"Mom!" I yell, running to the shore.

Callie grabs a branch and extends it. I'm helping now, my hands cold, wet.

Mom's splashing, screaming, "I hate my life."

"Please, Mommy. I love you best," I say. "Please. Grab the branch."

Mom finally seizes the branch and we haul her back to shore. She flops on the muddy ground, mascara ringing her eyes.

"It's okay, Mommy. Come on, let's get you cleaned up." She's a *mess*. I heft her to her feet. I've done it before, but never like this.

Mom says, "*You* made this happen, Ivy." She's so drunk I'm surprised she can speak.

Callie's trembling. She says, "I could run home, get my mom. She'll know what to do. We need an adult. Someone to take charge."

"No. Don't. It has to be a secret. Promise you won't tell. Promise!"

She pauses for, like, a hundred years. Then she says, "I promise."

But her promise wasn't enough for Mom. Edenville was over. Until now.

Now, Callie's snoring lightly right next to me, warm and close. It's three years later and we're not little girls anymore. The vodka bottle we drank from to play that stupid game earlier is on the bedside table. For my mother, the best way to deal with nights like this is oblivion. I run a finger along the side of the bottle, telling myself I'm not going to drink the burning liquid, let it rush down my throat. It's one thing to drink for fun. But no matter how dark I feel, I'm going to rise above the past. I'm going to let the darkness inside me fade. I imagine breathing in light. Focus on the *now*, Ivy.

Callie's here.

I kissed Kurt at BEneath.

New town.

New life.

New me.

ELEVEN DAYS EARLIER

Callie

It's the morning after and I wake feeling revolting. My head hurts, my mouth is furry and my back kills. I roll onto my side and bump into Ivy. I've turned upside-down in my sleep so the two of us are lying head to toe in Ivy's massive bed. I'm snarled up in bedsheets and my face is way too close to her feet, the toenails painted with bright pink polish. I'm reminded of all those sleepovers we had, whispering together late into the night. I shiver and sit up, but immediately wish I'd stayed lying down. The room spins and I remember tumbling into bed like a starfish tumbles through the ocean, if they even do that. Even my thoughts are confused, as if I'm still drunk.

I got *drunk* last night. I try to piece together the details. The fake ID, Kurt and Xander, dancing with Ivy, then me insisting we buy more drinks, vodka, paying for it, even, then drinking two disgusting shots in a row. After that, Kurt and Ivy. Dancing together, Kurt looking down at her. Then Ivy dancing with me again, pressed close, doing that thing I've seen other girls do when they get physical on the dance floor, all sexy and showy, turning on the guys. I've always thought it was slutty but it's fun.

I don't remember much more. Ivy saying she'd take me home. This bed, this comfortable bed.

I check my phone. Wow. It's not even six. I should get home, but I really don't feel like it. Even if Cosmo wakes her, Mom won't go into my room this early. She'll never know I've been gone.

Ivy sleeps while I shower in her huge ensuite bathroom; she sleeps while I put on my jeans and black sweater, leaving that slinky green dress hanging over the back of a chair; she sleeps while I scrub my face and brush my teeth, trying to remove the taste and smell of last night. Ivy's still asleep while I slip out of the house. I wander down toward the river, ignoring the way my head hurts and the way I'm dizzy, the dawn brightening around me.

At around six thirty, I text my mom: **Went out for a walk, up early. Lovely day**. It's weird to think she'll never know I snuck out last night.

My phone rings immediately. It's her. "Are you okay, Callie? I didn't hear you leave."

Since our fight, she's alternated between being over-concerned and distant. Clearly, right now she's over-concerned.

"You don't have to check up on me. I'm only going for breakfast."

I can tell from her exhalation of breath that she's annoyed. After a short pause she says, "How about I come with you?"

I'm way too hungover and tired, but I can't tell her that. Fortunately, Cosmo starts yelling and she says, "Sorry, my love, actually there's no way this morning. Next time, okay?"

My head throbs. "Okay, bye."

I text Ivy to tell her I've gone for a walk. She doesn't reply, so I assume she's still sleeping. I feel like we've switched places from that first day with her jogging and me slouching under the covers. I'm in the weirdest mood, antsy, awkward, headachy. I know it would be smart to go home and crawl into bed, but the thought of Mom hassling me about sleeping all day is too much.

Then I realize, it's Monday. The day of my interview at the gallery.

My phone rings again. "Where are you?"

"Rebecca?"

"We have plans, Cal."

"We do?"

"Hello? What's going on? I've been away a week but you've forgotten our reunion?"

Now I remember. Rebecca and I planned a ridiculously early reunion breakfast because she starts work at eight today. "Sorry. I, um, went out last night. I could be there in ten minutes?"

"Where'd you go?"

"To . . . BEneath."

"What? Without me? Callie!"

•

"I'm know. God, and I got drunk and —"

"Okay, can I have my friend back now? Whoever this is, get off Callie's phone." She's trying to make a joke of it but her voice is tense.

"You're mad at me."

"No. Who'd you go with?"

"Ivy."

"What? Ivy's back?"

"Um, yeah."

There's silence. We're both thinking it. She says, "Are you seriously doing this again?"

"It's not like that."

"What's it like then?"

"You were away."

"Oh my God, Callie. Forget breakfast."

"I'm already walking toward your house."

"Don't bother."

"Don't be mad. I can explain."

"What? I don't even want to hear it. Call me when you get over your girl-crush."

I say, "That's not what this is about."

"No?"

"Give me a break, Rebecca. I just went out to a bar with an old friend. You're being insane."

"Am I?" She pauses. "Maybe I am. I just . . . I figured . . . I thought we'd go to BEneath together the
first time. Is that dumb?"

"No . . ." It's my turn to backtrack. "It's me who's
sorry. I really am. I didn't even think."

She sucks in a breath. "That's what bothers me.
You didn't even think."

"Can I just come over?"

"I'm not really in the mood now. I've got to get
to work anyway."

"But how was your trip? How's your dad?"

"I'll call you later, okay? I'm not mad."

"You are."

"Okay. But I'll get over it. I'll call you later."

I sigh. I guess I should just go for the interview. My clothes are okay: normal, clean. I check
my face in the mirror in my phone and use a little
of the makeup Ivy gave me to make myself look
less tired. During the call, I'd started walking to
Rebecca's, but now I change direction. I head
across the bridge, passing the construction where
they're fixing a crack in the barrier. I amble by the
old hotel, with its pretty flower gardens and tacky
fountain that spurts water from fish-mouths. When

I arrive at the art gallery, I pull off my sweater and check the time. It's way too early for the gallery to be open. Wow, my brain is fried. I go into a new breakfast place next door to the gallery and eat bacon, eggs, hash browns and toast, and as I eat and drink bad coffee I feel myself come to life, a little.

By ten, I'm ready. I go inside to look for Ana. I'm told she's setting up in the Kids' Studio at the back, a small room furnished with three round tables and loads of small stools.

A smiley woman with dark hair pops her head out of the storage cupboard. "Callie? You're here about the job?"

I have a moment of panic. It's ridiculous to come for a job interview feeling like this, but I've been too foggy all morning to figure that out. "Hi, yes, that's me."

"Make yourself comfortable."

I sit on a stool and Ana smiles warmly at me. She has crow's feet round her eyes that make her look like she might be in her forties, but she has a surprisingly young voice. She says, "So, you enjoy art?"

"And creative writing."

While we talk, she folds piles of paper in several colours. "And you're good with children? I need someone to help clean up, help if anyone's struggling, hold down the fort, that type of thing. You'd never be on your own with the kids; you don't have to worry about that."

"That sounds okay to me. It sounds good." There's a screen on one wall and it comes on then, flashing an image of colours, weird shapes and some text that reads: *"Surrealism is merely the reflection of the death process*. Henry Miller."

Ana says, "Do you have any questions?"

I shake my head.

She says, "We run a varied program here. Sometimes we get a few kids, sometimes about twenty. We've got a session in half an hour. Do you want to do a trial run? We'll pay minimum wage."

"You want me to start now? Don't you need to check my resumé or references?" I might fall asleep at the table, but I don't want to let this opportunity pass by.

"I'll check all that later. If today goes well." She smiles again.

"Sure. Why not."

"Absolutely. Perfect—I *really* need the help." She rushes to the storage cupboard and hauls out a pile of blue paper. "Can't forget blue! We're making our own books today," she says. "Using our hands, our feet, our arms . . ."

"Sounds cool. Can I just let my mom know where I'm going to be?"

Ana nods.

I call Mom and say, "I got a job."

"What do you mean?"

"Well, a trial run, at least." I hear the smile in my voice.

"I knew you could—tell me! Is it one of the hotels?"

"It's at the gallery."

"That's wonderful! You never even mentioned that you dropped your resumé there. What does it involve?"

"I'll tell you later. I have to go. She wants me to do a trial run now."

"Your first job. That's big news. We'll have to celebrate."

"I haven't got it for sure yet."

"What's she paying you?"

"Mom, I have to go."

Once I'm off the phone, time speeds up. Parents arrive with children and in the end about fifteen kids sit looking adoringly up at Ana. We stitch pages together and I go round noticing who needs help. Each child makes a book titled *The Book of* . . ., followed by their name. They draw round their own hands and then write about themselves, filling in pictures and pages as they go. My headache fades. I sit down and help a tiny girl with a nest of black curls. I imagine Cosmo as a preschooler and feel an inner pinch. Maybe Mom has a point; I could do more stuff with him to help, and when he's older it might even be fun to hang out together.

It's near the end of the class when a couple of boys shriek and run over to Kurt, who has just arrived. He swings them up like they are monkeys, saying hello and kissing them on the cheeks. He nods at me and wanders over with his arms full, saying, "My little brothers, Sam and Adrian. I bring them when I work, then Dad picks them up."

They look nothing like him with their red hair, little snub noses and freckles. I say, "These two did a great job of their books." They squirm out of his arms and plop to the floor, looking pleased. A man arrives, nods hello to Kurt, and the boys rush off with him.

Kurt says, "So you work here now?"

Ana says, "Yes. She does. If everything checks out. Callie, email me later."

I smile as I say to Kurt, "Then I guess I do. Work here, I mean, since, um, about three hours ago."

"Cool." He lowers his voice. "You must feel . . . yeah . . . ill."

Ill? Oh, embarrassing. He saw me last night, drunk and silly. Except, he hardly saw me because he was looking at Ivy the whole time. "I don't normally. I mean," I sputter, "I don't really drink, um, ever."

"Not a big deal," he says.

But getting drunk is a big deal for me. I know in Kurt's world everybody drinks and parties, but it's not very *me*. I suddenly remember I saw Kurt kissing Ivy last night, the two of them entangled in the middle of the dance floor, and a couple of people whispering and texting about it. Ivy's big news already and she hasn't even started at our school yet.

Kurt breaks me out of my reverie. "Have you got a moment to grab a coffee when I'm done? In about an hour. There's a place next door. I . . . yeah . . . wanted to talk to you about something."

"Um . . . sure," I say.

After finishing up with Ana and the kids, and making sure the art room is spotless, I wander through the gallery and, because I'm a little early to meet Kurt, I take my time looking around the exhibition of Surrealist work. The paintings are like big red balloons would be at a funeral, strange and startling. I admire a painting of a rock stuffed into a hotel room, and one of a suitcase with a shadow of a hand resting upon it. I come to a complete stop at a painting that at first appears completely black until I make out a woman dressed in white lying slumped in the bottom corner. She makes me think of Ivy's mom. The weight of blackness presses down on her. I chew a hangnail on my thumb.

Kurt makes me jump when he says behind me, "I like this painting best."

"Yeah. I can see why."

"It's dark, but it's cool."

"Do you think I could do a piece on the exhibition? For *Flat Earth Theory*?" I ask.

"Good idea. Did you know the Surrealists used to play a game. Exquisite Corpse. One artist started the picture—drew the head. The next one drew the torso. Someone else finished it off—legs, feet. All on the same sheet of paper."

"Why's it called Exquisite Corpse?"

"It's from the word version of the game—*The exquisite corpse shall drink the new wine*. Something like that. Someone starts the story on a sheet of paper, folds it over. Hiding what they've written. The second person writes the next sentence, folds it over again. Someone else finishes it up. None of them know what the others have written until they read it out."

"It sounds, um, surreal."

"Yeah, look at these." He gestures to a glass case against one wall. There are about eight drawings of mixtures of strange heads and bodies, multiple legs, spots and swirls. He scuffs his sneaker against the floor. "So, yeah, about last night . . ." he says. "Did you and Xander . . . get to talk?"

"Xander's nice."

He studies the drawings again. A tiny frown crosses his face. Peeking out from beneath his black shirt is a leather cord with a silver dollar hanging from it. I say, "I like the necklace. I mean . . . I know guys don't call them necklaces, but . . ."

He smiles. "Yeah. Thanks."

"Nice. So, you wanted to talk. About the piece for the board? You haven't emailed the edits yet."

"No. It's nothing."

"Is it about Ivy, then? It's—"

"I'm being . . . whatever." He checks his phone. "I should go."

"Are you all right?"

"It's nothing," he says, and leaves me standing there alone.

At supper at home, Mom's distracted by Cosmo, who is "teething," um, yelling his head off. She tries to ask me about the job, but I don't get much of a chance to reply. Ivy texts asking me to come over. I head out, ignoring Mom's protests, telling her only that I'm going for another walk. I'm surprised she buys it, her radar *must* be on, but she must figure either that I wouldn't lie to her, or that I need the space.

I go straight to Ivy's, exhilarated by the fact Mom doesn't know where I am. Ivy's mom is out with Kevin so the house is still and quiet around us, like a feather duvet. I'm comforted by the silence. My house is always too loud with Cosmo wailing, or a gaggle of his baby friends around, filling up the living room, jumping in the Jolly Jumper and bashing away at noisy toys. Various mommies and their children drop by, people wanting my mom to sign books or to get involved with some charity or other. It's perfect, really: she's a successful children's book author and illustrator, and now she has a baby. Only problem is me, the teenager who doesn't quite fit the picture.

Ivy snaps me out of my sulk. Tells me to put some music on. As I scroll through, I realize I don't recognize any of the bands on her phone. They're all foreign and exotic sounding. I pick one at random, curious now. An accordion starts to play, backed up with heavy drums and some other instrument I can't identify. I dock the phone as a laconic voice hums, then says, *"They'll only let you down."* The voice switches to French. It's weird music, not something I'd associate with Ivy. She's lying on her sofa, skimming through a magazine, wearing a white tee and peach-coloured jeans. Her bare feet are crossed at the ankles.

The music plays for a moment or two longer, and she says, "That's me." I must look confused, because she continues, "Singing. I'm the singer."

I shut my eyes and listen. The girl singing can *really* sing but Ivy's the worst singer ever.

"There's no way, Ivy. You're tone-deaf."

She laughs. "True."

"It's not you?"

"Come, sit down." She doesn't raise her eyes from the magazine.

I flop on the sofa. She puts her feet in my lap.

"So you're not the one singing?"

"Caught out. I just wanted you to think—" She flicks her gaze to me. "That I was cool, or something."

"Of course I think that!"

"Sorry. It was stupid. I shouldn't pretend to be

someone I'm not. How about you give me a massage and then I'll give you one." She wiggles her foot.

"A foot massage?"

"What? My feet are clean."

Her toenails are painted five different tones of pink. I take one foot in my hand, press my thumbs into the flesh.

She says, "That feels good" and stretches out like a cat. "Sorry I'm being strange. Mom's drinking a lot already. Normally when we move we get a, well, grace period. Time off."

"That's awful." I sound naive but I don't know what else to say.

Ivy lets her head fall back on the arm of the couch and talks to the ceiling while I massage. "Kevin literally has no freaking idea how much Mom drinks. He thinks she's fun—a live-wire, makes him feel young, whatever. And Dad's too busy being a swanky investment banker to give a flying—"

"Are you in touch with him?"

She lifts her head. "He sends money. In his head that makes up for it. He remarried, a twenty-two-year-old, so I guess he doesn't need me. Gross. Like, so predictable of him." Her phone interrupts her. She checks the screen. "Oooh, it's Kurt."

She yanks her feet away and jumps up. Her voice suddenly husky, she answers the call, heading out of the room, closing the door. I check through my own phone, waiting, looking at some photos Tilly posted of her family at the cabin.

When Ivy comes back she says, "We're going out on the boat tomorrow. You're coming."

As if Mom knows what Ivy's just said, she phones. I say to Ivy, "Hang on."

Mom says, "Hey, Callie my love. Where are you? Why don't I meet you? We could walk together. Cosmo's sleeping. Your dad's here. I've got my coat on already."

I feel a pang for when Mom and I used to spend time together. It's followed by a spool of anxiety that she'll figure out where I am. As far as I can tell, I'm still *forbidden* to see Ivy.

"Actually, Mom, I'm just coming down the street now. I'll see you at home." I get off the phone and say to Ivy, "I'm sorry. I gotta go. Mom needs help with Cosmo." Lies get easier and easier. "I'll call you about the boat. I don't think I should go, though."

Ivy stands to hug me goodbye. "You're coming."

"Okay. I definitely am."

Mom's sitting on the couch when I get back, waiting. "Want me to make you a cold drink? Lemonade from real lemons?"

She still thinks I'm a little girl. She really doesn't get it.

"No, thanks. How's Granny?"

"Same. I don't think the fall is causing this confusion. I actually think she fell because she had a mini-stroke or something. I'm going to call the doctor about her again tomorrow."

"A mini-stroke?"

"We'll see. I'm not saying that's it. Try not to worry. Sure you don't want lemonade?"

"I'm pretty tired, Mom. I got up early." *I've been awake for a hundred thousand hours.*

"I wanted to hear about work. About you. I haven't seen you much."

"Yeah." There's no way she'll let me go on the boat tomorrow, so I lie. "I've got work all day tomorrow too."

"At the gallery? Why don't Cosmo and I come down and see you."

"Um, no." I panic. "No, I mean, yes, please, but not right away. Give me a few days to settle in. Please?"

She nods. "Of course." She's still sitting on the couch, but now she's at the edge of it, hands on her knees. "About Ivy, I do mean it. I don't want you seeing her."

I force myself to stay calm. "Yeah, I know. I haven't."

"You wouldn't lie to me?"

"Mom, what is this? No, I wouldn't lie. Can I go to bed now? I've got work tomorrow and I'm tired."

She appraises me, then nods again. "Okay, sweetheart. Sleep well."

On the way up the stairs, I'm fuming. Mom needs to take her foot off the pedal.

FIVE

JULY 31ST

Kurt

Xander returns with one foam cup of coffee in each hand. Seeing Mrs. Foulds is gone, he puts one cup on the table next to me. He sips from the one meant for her. I guess he figures she's not returning anytime soon. His cell beeps — beeps again.

Switch it off.

He checks the screen, silences it. The silence is worse.

He says, as if to reassure himself, "They'll tell us when they know something."

I say, "The doctor left with Mrs. Foulds. I didn't even get to ask anything. Man, people don't survive shit like that."

I'm not even sure he's heard until he says, "Take it easy."

I fiddle with the remote but it doesn't work. The TV keeps playing the same channel. Xander paces the corridor. Flat expression on his face. He could be on a grim hike. My head slams like the worst hangover.

I rub the top of my nose. It's a gesture from my dad. Not my birth-dad. He died when I was six months old—cancer. That was when my birth-mom started drinking, apparently. This gesture is from my adopted dad. Sometimes when I walk into that huge kitchen, my brothers scrapping on the floor, and Mom turns to me with a plate of fresh-cooked bacon, eggs and rye toast, I split in two. The person I was before they adopted me. And the person I am now. Took me years to stop being scared that my adopted family would make me go back to my birth-mom. I used to dream of houses flooding, cracks appearing in the walls. I tried to explain it to Xander once. He took it in, the way he does. Solid. But I'm not sure he got it.

When I visit my birth-mom, I'm a little kid. All over again. At the same time, I'm me. Able to protect myself. Ivy recognized this. Somehow, she understood.

I think about what she told me on the boat. There's something about vulnerable that makes me go soft. She sat on the prow, the water behind her like a blue canvas. Told me she wanted to start over. Said Callie was her "rock."

I said, "Callie's like Xander—self-sufficient. More than she knows. They seem a good match."

Ivy said, "You'll help me start over."

"You don't need my help."

She laughed. "I don't need anyone."

She sure knew how to flirt.

Shit. I just used the past tense. But she can't be dead. Not Ivy.

TEN DAYS EARLIER

Ivy

I pick at the paint chipping from my bedroom window frame. Kevin didn't get this room redone, although the room he shares with Mom is spandangly new. I murmur into my phone, "It's been a while, Diego."

He says, "I thought you'd call."

"You miss me, then." Guys just need it told to them sometimes—it's not like emotions are their strong point.

He's quiet.

I flick a paint chip to the floor, grind it with my bare toes. "It sucks here without you," I say. "I forgive you, you know."

"Shit, Ivy . . ."

"I gotta go." I press End before he can answer. Always, always leave them wanting more.

I start my morning exercises, following the 60/60/60 routine my online CrossFit program sets me. Sixty burpees. Sixty lunges. Sixty sit-ups. Then I listen to a podcast about living your best life. The speaker is a woman, about thirty, gorgeous, funny, in control, just about exactly who I'm gonna be one day.

❋

Mom's downstairs making waffles. "Hey, sugar," she says. She's trussed up in a pink apron. Her hair is loose. For a moment I let myself believe and I say all cutesy, "Hey, Mommy."

She opens the waffle maker and spoons in some mix. It sizzles. "Don't you just love it here, Ivy?"

I shrug one shoulder.

"Kevin wants to take the two of us for supper somewhere elegant." Her deep red lipstick frames her smiling mouth. She's stylish when she wants to be, like a photograph from a magazine. I get it from her. Not that I'm boasting or anything. I just have a feel for clothes, hair, makeup. I could go into that, I suppose. I'm meant to be planning all that— planning a future.

"Blueberries?" she asks.

"Sure."

"What are you doing today?" She hovers over the waffle maker.

"Heading to Kurt's boat."

"Kurt?"

"Just some guy. He's cute." I twirl a strand of my hair around my index finger. "Are you okay?"

"Why wouldn't I be okay?" she says, all shiny like a sequin.

"Just, you know. Moving. Kevin."

"Kevin's a wonderful guy."

"If you say so."

"Don't spoil this, Ivy."

I swallow. Hard. My throat hurts. I think over the podcast. *When the world tries to get you down, just hold yourself up higher. Fill yourself with light.*

She opens the waffle maker and tips the waffle onto my plate. It smells buttery and sweet. "God, can't you just be grateful?"

"I am, Mom. Sorry."

"You should be. It's not every girl who gets waffles made by her mom for breakfast. I never did. My mom was too busy travelling the world, acting in movies to make me waffles. No time for a kid, oh no, just pack up your stuff and follow along . . . but I made time for you."

I've heard it all before, the way she says it with no

trace of irony—like, doesn't she *see*? I try to pull her rant-train back on track. "The waffles look delicious."

"Of course they do."

We're there. Light fills me. And now I have a waffle to eat too.

Kevin walks in. "Hello there, my girls. Super duper. Breakfast all together?" He's the only person I've ever met who actually grins. With his red velvet housecoat and potbelly he's too gross to contemplate. He says, "Circling the wagons!"

Mom smiles broadly. "How it should be. Right, Ivy?"

I nod. "Absolutely." *Happy families are made up of happy individuals.* "Absolutely," I say again.

Callie

Rebecca's at my front door. "Surprise," she says. "I thought I'd come see you."

I give her a hug and say, "You're not mad anymore?" She has a blue streak in her hair. I add, "Um, you did your hair while you were camping?"

"Yesterday after work."

"Sorry I didn't call back."

"S'okay. I wasn't really speaking to you anyways." Rebecca is wiry and muscly. She's on the track team, cross-country ski team, swim team, and is about as outdoorsy as it gets.

"So, you got physical with nature?" I say as she follows me into the house. "Pitched a tent? Hiked with bears? Posted stuff on the Internet?"

She laughs and slides up onto the kitchen counter. "Hi, Mom-Two," she says to my mom.

"Hey, sweetheart. You had a nice time with your dad?"

"It's always nice when Melissa's not there." Rebecca calls Melissa slutbag when my mom's not around.

Mom juggles Cosmo on her hip and Rebecca coos at him, "Hey, baby. You got bigger!"

He smiles at her.

"He loves me!" she says.

"'Kay, no more Cosmo." I yank her off the counter. "We're going outside."

"We are?"

I nod. "We are." I grab my bag.

When we get outside I break it to her. "Don't be mad."

"What?"

"You won't believe it."

"What?" She's sardonic. "You're killing me."

"Seriously. I'm going out on a boat today with Kurt and Xander."

"No! How come?"

"They asked me. Okay, that's not true. Kurt asked Ivy." I glance at Rebecca to see if Ivy's name is an okay topic of conversation.

"Ivy?" she says, and pulls a face.

"Rebecca, we're not kids anymore."

"What does that mean?" Her cheeks grow red.

"Becs, this isn't about Ivy. This is about me. Isn't it cool? I'm actually doing something cool with my summer."

"Is hanging out with me not considered cool, then?"

"I don't mean that."

"So when are you going on this boat?"

"Um, like, now."

"Now?"

"Yeah. But I'm going to pretend to Mom that

I'm hanging out with you and then that I'm going to work."

"Oh, okay." I can tell she's trying to stop herself from crying. Tough as a daylily, tender as a daisy.

"I didn't *know* you were coming over," I say.

We've walked a little way from my house and we're standing outside Ivy's. Ivy comes out.

Rebecca lifts a hand in a fake wave and grimaces. "Hi, Ivy."

Ivy squeals and rushes to hug Rebecca. "Amazing! So good to see you. Love the hair."

Rebecca disentangles herself. She says, "Course you do. Right, Callie, I'm just going to go."

"Becs, don't. Come with us."

Ivy pitches in. Trying to cover the tension. "Yes, come too. Kurt won't mind."

I wish Rebecca would just relent, relax into it, but she glares at me. "I'd love to, but I've got stuff to do. See you later."

Ivy grabs my hand. "See you, Becs. We should go, Callie."

Rebecca glances at Ivy's hand holding mine.

"I'll call you later," I say.

Kurt pulls up in his dad's car. There's no time

for guilt about Rebecca because Ivy is tugging me
away.

Xander and I chat together at the bow of the boat.
He's easy to talk to and he asks me questions about
my life, about my family. I answer, stunned that
I'm even here, on this boat, free on the water, the
sky open above me. The sun warms my face. I finish eating some chips and tidy the empty bag away.

"Come on," says Xander, "I'll show you how to
drive this thing." He talks me through steering,
which is easy, and soon I'm holding the wheel,
guiding the boat in a long straight line. I can see
the attraction of the water, how the boat feels
like it's mine as it glides forward. I'm reminded
of my dad reading to me when I was a child, the
first time I heard the epic poem about Odysseus'
extraordinary sea adventures.

I used to relate to Penelope, the one who stayed at
home and waited for the return, but now I'm Odysseus
himself. I'm thinking about how he was strapped to
the mast of his ship so he could survive the Sirens,

women who live in the ocean and lure sailors to their death with their songs, when Xander speaks. "Nice to be on the boat, hey?"

"It sounds weird, but I was just imagining being a great sea explorer, there being gods and monsters on the next island. I've always been really into *The Odyssey*. My dad used to read it to me as a kid. Not really kid-appropriate. I never understood everything he was saying, but I loved it all the same."

Kurt sticks his head round from the side of the boat. He says, "Beautiful water today. Might swim later."

"The Sirens calling you?" I pause, not sure he'll know what I'm talking about. God, I'm such a nerd.

"Yep," he says, "strap me to the mast." So he gets the reference. He says, "What? You think editors don't read?"

"No, I just . . ."

He laughs. "I always wanted to go to Greece. My birth-dad was Greek. If he hadn't died, I dunno. Greece seems like a cool place. Who knows, if we'd moved there when I was born, stuff like that. Kid-fantasy stuff." He loops his thumbs in his jeans. "All that to say, I read Homer. It stuck in my head. So, you look like you've got a good handle on the boat. Xander's teaching you to steer?"

"It's not as hard as driving a car. Do you know I drove the instructor's car into a fire hydrant in my second Driver's Ed class?"

"I heard the rumour," he says. "Didn't know it was you."

"I'm the worst driver ever."

Xander laughs. "You should have told me that before, Captain!"

Kurt jumps down so he's standing level with me. I stare out at the horizon. Xander takes a beer from a cooler and leans against the rail, the sun on his face. He closes his eyes.

Ivy comes down next to Kurt and laces her fingers with his. A tiny pulse jumps in my chest. I think of those hospital machines that show the heart flatlining and then jumping to life again.

Xander says, without opening his eyes, "Who's hungry?"

"Definitely," says Ivy. "What have we got?" She rests her head against Kurt's chest.

I watch his face as he puts his chin on the top of her head and quickly strokes her hair.

"It's all there," says Xander. "Bread, ham, cheese, beer."

Ivy moves away, stands next to Xander now and smiles at me. "We'll get it ready," she says. She busies herself lifting a bag from the cooler.

I glance once more at Kurt. Our eyes meet. Awkward. I say to Ivy, "Let's go down below deck, we can prep everything there."

The boat stays steady, perfectly on course as we make our way into the tiny galley. Ivy smells of sugar and vanilla. She passes me the bread and I lay the slices on a small counter. The boat jolts and she stumbles against me.

"Sorry," I say.

She laughs, then says, "Kurt's nice, hey?"

"I guess so."

"You never thought about him, you know, like that?"

"I don't know. He's never been interested." I press my lips together to try and stop myself sighing too loudly.

She says softly, "What?"

"You just make it all look so easy."

"Easy?"

"Just . . . guys, life."

She squirts mayo on the bread. I plop down slices of cheese and ham.

"Guys are like dogs."

I laugh. "I didn't expect you to say that."

She squeezes my hand. "Let's eat, then I'll tell you all about how to get the hang of men."

That evening, Dad hovers at my bedroom door. "Calliope," he says. He's the only one ever to still call me by my full name.

I'm in the middle of texting Ivy. I glance at him.

His lips move as if he's considering what to say, then he blurts, "I hear Ivy's back in town."

"Did Mom put you up to this?"

"I know it's not easy. I remember being your age. Things were a little . . . a little simpler then, it seems."

"Dad, I'm fine. Really. I'm not . . . whatever you think. I'm just . . . fine." I chuck down my cell and go to kiss him on the cheek. He smells freshly showered.

My cell starts ringing.

He ruffles my hair and says, "Never mind. You answer that." He gives me an impenetrable look, then ambles away.

I return to the bed, flop down, *a fish out of water*, and answer my cell. It's Ivy. Her voice is bubbly, cheerful. "Kurt's asked us to a party at his house tomorrow," she says. "Tell your parents you're staying the night at mine."

The line replays in my head: *A fish out of water*. I ignore it.

"Sounds good," I say. Maybe I can tell my parents I'm going out with Rebecca. Thinking about Rebecca makes my mouth a little dry. I should call her.

"What are you gonna wear?" Ivy asks.

"I don't know. Any suggestions? I wish I could come over now and raid your clothes."

"Come over."

"I can't." I've already been out all day. I flip onto my tummy. "I'm going to see my granny in the morning. Apparently she's not doing great. Then I'm working in the afternoon."

"Can I come?"

"To the gallery?"

"No, to see your granny."

"Why? I mean, well, what for?"

"Just to be *nice*. Don't sick people like having visitors? And old people too. Old, sick people . . . Plus, I'm kinda interested in this running-away war bride thing."

"I guess so. She loves talking about that. Okay, yeah. Around ten?"

"Sure." She says, "Now, Kurt's party. I'm gonna wear something short. And sexy."

"And white, right?"

"Right." She laughs. Throaty.

"I'll have to figure out how to get Mom to let me go." A reckless feeling shivers through me.

"What's up?" Ivy says into the sudden silence.

"I dunno. Nothing. It'll be fine."

"Sure. See you tomorrow. Can't wait."

SIX

JULY 31ST

Kurt

I glance at the black coffee. I can't drink it. Inertia. I don't like it about myself, wish I could be more decisive, but when things get tough I blank out. Freeze.

It was the only way to protect myself when I was a little kid. When my mom tore up the world around me. There's no way to explain to most people, people like Callie or Xander, that life can be so bad sometimes the only way to deal with it is to pretend none of it's happening. Or, the opposite. Life can be so good, the possibility of the future so awesome that the only way to protect yourself from ruining it is to sit back. Let the opportunity slide by.

I think about Callie. Once at an editorial meeting, she told me she wanted to write a profile of her grandmother. I said, "I dunno. High-school kids read this, remember?"

"Yeah. She was a high-school kid too. Fell in love during high school and moved here, middle of nowhere, dusty train ride, got out of the train to meet her soldier in the backwater of Edenville. She wore a dress made from a parachute at their wedding. You're telling me that's not interesting for a high-school kid?"

"Cool it, Callie."

"I don't need to cool it. You just need to remember the whole world isn't football and girls."

"That's what I'm all about?" I joked. "Football and girls?"

"No, I didn't mean it like that."

"You didn't?"

She tucked her pen behind her ear. "Guess I did."

I laughed. Put up my hands in surrender. "That's right, all I care about is football and girls. You do the piece."

She nodded, smiled. "Good."

Xander sits opposite me in the hospital waiting room. He repeats from a few minutes ago, "Take it easy." I realize he's not talking to me at all, more saying it to himself. In TV shows about hospitals, everything is fast. Vital. Pulse of life and drama. Here, in real life, the place is stagnant. It reeks of cleaning fluid. Glares with eerie yellow light. Echoes with the cry of a patient from a faraway room, the soft pad of nurses' shoes, the ring of a phone, the blurting of the TV.

A show about car crashes comes on. A show I would normally love. A race-car spins three times. Smashes against the buffers. Explodes into a ball of fire and light. A man crawls from the wreckage, blackened and screaming. I sit and watch. It's sick but I'm rooted to the spot. Watching the next crash, and the next.

And then I hear a strangled sound. Xander is crying. He presses his face into his hands. Sobs shake his shoulders.

I look away. Powerless.

NINE DAYS EARLIER

Ivy

"Here we are," Callie says. She uses her key to get into her grandmother's apartment.

"You okay?" I whisper.

"Sure. Ish."

I squeeze her arm. Her granny sits in a large floral armchair, her eyes all dreamy. When she sees us, she reaches for the teapot. "Hey, girls. You're here. How lovely. Callie, Poppet. And you're . . ."

Callie says, "This is Ivy."

"Ivy. I'd never forget."

Callie says, "Let me do that, Granny."

Her grandmother refuses and pours tea. Adds milk. Hands me a china cup. It's cold. Gross. It's all a bit gross — old people aren't really my thing, but the podcast I listened to yesterday mentioned that *the best way to grow as a person is to step outside your comfort zone.* I'm totally outside it right now.

I say, "I like your place. Roses. Super pretty." I'm talking about the wallpaper. Old people. I don't have much experience but they're not rocket science.

Callie's granny says, "I remember when I had a rose garden. You like roses?"

"Of course."

Callie's granny goes to put her cup on the table, but misses the edge. The cup drops and shatters. Tea splashes everywhere. "Oh," she cries. "I just don't know what's *wrong* with me today."

Callie's eyes get shiny. She's completely paralyzed. Even though I don't want to, I imagine what Callie would do and I jump up to grab a cloth from the kitchen. I wipe up, then find a broom, swiftly clear up the pieces.

"You're a lovely girl, Ivy." She seems to drift again. Then she says, "But how's your poor mother, dear? Terrible for you."

No fricking way.

Callie says, "Granny!"

"Yes, darling?"

Callie glances at me. Apologizing with her eyes. *Thanks for nothing.*

Her granny slips to a new subject. "When I was growing up in England, I had a friend like you, Ivy. She was wonderful."

Light is seeping from me. Callie swore she'd told no one—so now who else knows?

"She, my friend, passed away when we were young. It was so sad. I thought I'd never . . . She and I planned to come here together. She was in love with a soldier, like me. Ah, we had everything to live for. But enough gloominess. What are your summer plans, girls?"

Callie's looking at the floor.

I say, "Oh, the usual."

And the conversation meanders on. Callie's granny slides from brisk and cheerful to strange and confused. At one point she sees a kitten dart across the floor. She asks me at least three more times about my mom. Each time, I feel the light inside me diminish further. Each time, Callie sends me an apologetic look and asks her granny to talk about something else.

Finally, finally it's time to go.

When we get out the door, Callie gushes, "I didn't tell her. Not everything. I glossed over it. I was only a kid. She would never have said anything

just now if she wasn't so . . . just recovering. Mom
thinks she might have had a mini-stroke. Granny's
just not herself."

"You swear you didn't tell anyone else?"

"I swear."

I can forgive. I can let go. *Holding on to rage is like
holding on to a burning stick* — my own self will be the
only one damaged by anger. I struggle but I manage to say, "It's no big deal."

"Really?"

"Really." Okay, so I don't mean it just yet, but I
will when I've let the anger drain away. I imagine
bathwater emptying, dark feelings swirling down
from my body. I *can* trust Callie. I convince myself.
Yes, I can trust her.

She says, "You seem, I dunno, upset."

"Can we talk about it later? I've got loads to do
before I get ready for Kurt's party tonight."

"Ivy, I'm sorry."

"We'll talk later. Promise."

My hair's loose. I'm in a tight white dress. Toned.

At least all those sit-ups earlier were worth it. I remind myself as I head out the door: *I'm a beautiful person.* Xander honks his horn, ready to drive to Kurt's house out of the city somewhere. I wave to him and his glance flicks down my body as he stammers a hello. Yeah, yeah. He's trying so hard to be a nice boy but I know what he's thinking. Some other gangly guy with vile teeth lounges shotgun. Introduces himself as Greg and goggle-eyes me with no attempt to hide it.

I get in the back seat. Light up a cigarette. Text Callie. She appears at her front door and slinks down the road. Checks over her shoulder as she climbs into Xander's car.

I say, "Super pretty. Nice gold-dust on your cheeks."

"You're okay about this morning?"

I put an arm around Callie's shoulder. She smells of baby soap. I pass her the cigarette I'm smoking. Yes, I know I want to quit, but now isn't the right time. Callie doesn't smoke, but she takes the cigarette anyway. Drags too hard and makes her eyes water. I grab her hand and she tangles her fingers in mine. She's not looking at me now but gazing out the window on her side. Her hand is warm, a bit sweaty. Friends again.

Xander turns down the music and starts telling Greg some story he's read about a sixteen-year-old who's changing the world—she's fighting for women's rights and was nominated for, but didn't win, a Nobel Peace Prize.

Callie says quietly to me so they can't hear in the front, "It seems impossible to be sixteen and doing something so amazing."

I say, "Why do you say stuff like that?"

"I just look at the world and figure I can't—"

"You need to unlock your potential." I wonder if she'd be interested in some of my favourite podcasts.

She says, "I'm just so . . . stuck in my ways. I'm trying." She adds, "Do I just chuck the cigarette butt out the window?"

"You're picking up trashy habits from me."

She giggles. "I'm trying to."

Greg says, "What are you two whispering about?"

"Girl stuff," I say.

"Tell us. We love that."

I say, "I bet you do."

Callie

We drive until the city is far behind us, and then turn up a long gravel road that trails into a cluster of trees surrounded by barns and silos. The sound of grit spraying up silences our chatter.

As I step outside the car, I can't help but notice the fresh, warm prairie air. Although it's past nine thirty when we arrive, the sky is alive with the setting sun: purples and pinks, oranges and blues. A line bursts into my head: *When the sky is laid bare, put a hand on my skin, let me in, let me in.*

Ivy grabs me. "See. Fun." She moves away to look at the gigantic house. Our city doesn't have a lot of houses as fancy as this and I've never been inside one like it before. I'm whirly-happy-dizzy from the cigarettes and the buzz of being here. Wow, my life just keeps looking up.

Kurt's there, slapping Xander on the back, saying a cheerful hello to Ivy, the other guy and me. His eyes fix on mine and I try to read his expression. Ivy tilts her face up and he bends to kiss her. It's a quick kiss, but I see her hand slip round his neck, comfortable and sexy. With shocking force, I wish for that kiss. I make a vow to myself: I need to find someone to kiss me like that. Maybe this party is the place to do it.

The house is full of people who are drinking and laughing and dancing. The entranceway is bigger than my whole downstairs floor at home, and it has a grand staircase leading up each side. The walls are papered gold and silver. There are a few large, awkward sculptures around — ugly black things. As we drift into the massive family room, I spot three TVs on different walls, heaps of trendy computer gadgets and speaker systems, and a fully stocked bar where the man who picked up Sam and Adrian from Artstarts is shaking a drink mixer with flare. No way. Kurt's *dad* is the bartender.

He yells over the loud music, "Kurt? Your mom called. She and the boys are happy at Grandma's. She says to have fun." He calls to Xander, "Give up your keys, or promise not to drink."

"Sure, Mr. Hartnett. Here they are. I'd like a beer." He hands over his keys.

Two thoughts come to me at once: First, *I have no way to get home*. Second, *Ivy knew we were staying over.*

She loops an arm around my waist. "You figured out we're staying the night? I brought you one of my T-shirts to sleep in."

"Ivy, Mom'll kill me. I *can't* stay. They're expecting me home after a movie. I told them I was with Rebecca. I said I'd be back at midnight."

Ivy squeezes me. "Rebecca? Why? I *told* you to tell them you're staying the night at mine. Come on, have a drink. Let's enjoy."

"You don't understand."

"What? Why lie about Rebecca?"

I can't tell Ivy that Mom has forbidden me to hang out with her. I'm still stressing that Granny might tell Mom that Ivy came over earlier, even though I managed, when Ivy was in the wash-room, to ask Granny not to tell. Granny gave me a long look and said, "Careful, Callie."

Ivy repeats, "Why lie about Rebecca?"

A new thought sneaks into my head: *Live a little, Callie, stop stressing. Have fun.* I say, feeling giddy, "Don't worry about it. I'll see what I can do."

I text Mom: **Becs wants me to stay the night.**

Is that OK? My heart is high in my chest. What if she says no?

But she texts back: **You don't have a toothbrush!**

— **She can lend me one.**

— **K then. Be good. Love you.**

— **Thanks!**

I send the text and then my phone dies. Out of battery. Crap. Mom'll hate that, but it's done now. I push away my nerves and turn to smile at Kurt's dad.

He says, "Who are you two lovely ladies?"

Kurt says, "This is Callie. From *Flat Earth Theory*, remember?"

Ivy reaches out her hand. "And I'm Ivy. I'd love one of whatever it is you're making."

At some point during the party, the crowds have thinned out. Kurt's dad, who vigilantly checked every kid before they left, gives Kurt a high-five and retreats upstairs. A couple of guys who drank loads are passed out in various bedrooms. Ivy is sitting on a huge leather sofa playing some race-

car computer game with Xander and Greg. I head
to the kitchen and start clearing up, filling the sink,
letting the soapsuds warm my hands as I wash
glasses. Music comes from a speaker somewhere,
strange high-pitched music, like nothing I've
heard before. Alien. I think of worlds other than
our own, alternative universes, faraway planets.
And then I think of Kurt. The way he caught my
eye earlier.

The way he kissed Ivy at BEneath.

The reckless way I'm feeling.

There's a scream. I spin round. It's Ivy and
she's standing on the couch, play-fighting with
Greg. I turn away and dip my hands back into
the suds.

Kurt enters the kitchen, carrying a trash bag. I
stop washing glasses and look at him. For a moment
he doesn't notice me because he's emptying a dirty
plate and then watching Ivy and Greg, who collapse
shouting and laughing. A tall brunette wearing a
skimpy outfit drapes herself over Xander. She's
giving Ivy death glares, but Ivy's way too caught
up in the game to care about anything. She yells,
"Don't even try it" at the screen.

I sense Kurt looking at me and I think about him and Ivy. A secret feeling crawls through my chest.

Kurt says, "You don't need to be doing this. I've got it."

"It's no problem. I'm enjoying myself actually. It's weird but I like clearing up and this music is cool."

"It's my dad. It's an mp3 of him playing the saw." Kurt explains, "If you take a regular saw and then pass a special bow over it, it sounds like that."

"A regular saw," I repeat. As I do, the sound takes on a new intensity. Alone, I would close my eyes and enjoy it fully. Instead I say, "Your dad seems pretty cool."

"Yeah. He knows how things are."

I step back a little so my back is pressed against the sink. Warm water seeps through the waistband of my jeans. I say, "My mom and dad had a baby recently. My brother. He cries a lot."

"You like having him around?"

"Um . . . honestly? He makes me feel jealous. Stupid. I'm jealous of a *baby*."

"You'll get used to him."

"I might do."

He laughs. "Probably. Aren't babies supposed to be kinda adorable?"

"You'd think."

Ivy yells over at us, "Don't work so hard, guys — we can do it later."

Kurt turns to pick up another beer can, heaves up the trash bag and says to her, "We're nearly done." Then to me, "Better get to it."

Ivy shrieks with laughter at something Greg's said. She yells, "When you two are finished being boring, come party with us. I've got a great idea."

I head to the empty front area, that echoing space, tidying a few last things before joining the others.

Kurt walks back into the house. He bumps into me and says softly, "Callie?"

In the semi-shadow, I say, "What?"

A drunk girl appears at the top of the stairs and says, almost to herself, "Which way again?" then disappears through a different door.

Kurt says, "So, we're friends. You and me?"

"Sure."

"I just . . . I—"

Ivy yells out, "Callie, where are you?"

I say to Kurt, "Course we're friends. What's up?"

"Nothing."

"You're allowed to relax a little," I say. "It's your party, after all. Come on—we're done cleaning."

I head to the living room, thinking he's going to follow, but he doesn't. It's smoky from cigarettes but there's another smell underneath, sweet and exotic. Pot. Xander and Greg are both sitting on the leather sofa, and Ivy has moved to sit on a nearby loveseat. She shoots me a look. I sit next to her and she hands me a bottle; it's some blue, sweet cooler. I take a few sips then hand it back to her.

"Yuck."

She says, "I can't believe you cleaned everything."

"You know what I'm like."

Her eyes are a little bloodshot. "Do I?"

"Course you do."

She squeezes my hand. "Course I do."

"So, what's the great idea—remember, earlier you said you had a great idea?"

She raises her voice. "Xander, Greg, turn that squeaky crap off. Let's play a game. Where's

Kurt?" She looks around then presses close to me.
She says, "No problem, we'll start without him."
As she says this, Kurt comes into the room. "Yay,
baby," she says. "Come sit next to us."

He obliges, so now I'm squashed with the whole
left side of my body pressed against him and Ivy
against me on my right.

Ivy says, "Let's play the game."

Greg stares at Ivy like he wants to eat her. She
doesn't seem to notice. I realize that he's just rolled
a joint. He lights it.

"Sure," he says. "We could play a game. Why
not?"

Ivy giggles, stoned. She reaches forward and
Greg passes her the joint.

"So," Ivy says, "you have to confess something."

Greg says, "This is a *girl's* game. What, confess
what? Like, I think Ivy's hot?"

Ivy laughs like Greg has said something really
funny. I feel Kurt tense beside me. She reaches over
me into Kurt's shirt pocket to pull out his cigarettes.
Her voice slurs. "Cute, Greg. Callie's turn. Come on,
Callie. You must have things to confess."

I think about Granny and how I feel bad that

I wasn't there when she fell. Is that the kind of thing to confess? I wonder what the others are thinking. It's exciting to be like this: unsure of what's going to happen next. And a little scary.

Ivy cuts in. "Okay, God, you guys need to get into this. I confess that I like Kurt."

Greg says, "Big news." He adds, "I confess that I stole this pot from my big brother."

Ivy nods. "That's more like it."

Everyone goes quiet again.

Very quietly, Ivy says, "I guess it has to be my turn again. I confess that I killed someone."

Greg says, "You're funny."

Ivy half closes her eyes. She murmurs, "I'm serious. Her name was Isabel Cabezas. It was an accident, of course, but it never felt like that. It felt like murder. It's so hard to live with what I've done."

My stomach clenches. Isabel Cabezas. Isabel's ID card is in my jacket pocket, my jacket that's hanging in the closet in Kurt's hallway.

Kurt says, "Are you serious?"

God. She's *serious*.

Xander says, "What happened?"

Ivy widens her eyes, leans forward a little, spools
us all in. "Izzy was older than me. We were best
friends. Like sisters. She was driving her motorbike. I was on the back . . ." Ivy is speaking in a soft
voice, and it's as if all of us have ceased to exist.
"Isabel was going fast. She was angry about something that I'd told her. I had my arms around her
waist. When she took a corner, we hit the curb and
both of us flew through the air. I landed on the
grass but she . . . just . . . I crawled over to her,
screaming her name. She died in my arms. It's why
Mom and I came back here, why we left Kansas
City—we had to get away."

We're all silent. I try to imagine Ivy lying on the
ground, her best friend dying in her arms. "God,
Ivy," I murmur.

Ivy says, "If I hadn't made her angry, she wouldn't
have been driving so fast. She wouldn't have died.
It's my fault." She sits as still as a porcelain figurine,
her eyes glassy with tears.

I come to my senses. I have to *do* something. I
have to get her out of here before she says any more.
If I were a better friend I would have stopped this
earlier. I stand. "Ivy, let's go."

The three guys stare at me. I say, "Kurt, which room can we sleep in?"

To my relief, Ivy gets up and follows, quiet and distracted, moving like she's walking through deep water.

Kurt leads us up to one of his brothers' rooms on the second floor. He mumbles a good night and I shut the door. There's a small lamp on in the room and it's cozy, so different from the cavernous living room with its dark shadows of Ivy's story.

Ivy collapses onto the bed, grabs my hand and tugs me down. I fall next to her. "Callie," she says, and giggles. The mood shifts. She runs a finger from the corner of my eye to the edge of my mouth. "Let me kiss you."

"I'm . . ." My tongue touches my top lip.

She smiles. "You know you want to."

Her mouth is very close. She smells of alcohol. Of pot. Those things she said, those awful things. "You're high, and upset," I say pulling away. "We'll talk tomorrow."

Her eyes glitter. She says, "Did you miss me?"

"You know I did."

She closes her eyes. She's asleep within seconds. I switch out the light, my mind a tornado. Ivy. Isabel. I'm left in a too-warm bedroom with nothing but the image of two girls flipping through the air, one of them to her death.

SEVEN

JULY 31ST

Kurt

Xander gets up from the waiting room sofa and walks off down the corridor without looking back at me. There'll be a story about this car accident for *Flat Earth Theory*, but it's one I could never write. I'm too close to this. I think about Callie and Ivy again, the party at my house, the things Ivy said when she was high.

There's something about getting high that I love. I should say *loved*. I don't do it anymore. I was about fourteen when I first got into all that, started being the guy at every party. I was younger than most of them, but I've always looked older than I am. One party sticks in my head. A bunch of seniors, drinking, some college guys. I got myself a beer and worked on getting fucked up. Two beers, three, four. A few shots. I was staggering drunk. Then I took a pill, began rushing. I was feeling great until I saw my birth-mom. At the party. Holding hands with an older guy, deep in conversation. She saw me as I saw her. The moment that changes your life. Changed mine. It was the look in her eyes—sure there was shame, guilt, anger, remorse—but the biggest emotion I read on her face was resignation. Resignation because her kid was *just like her*.

Xander returns. Sits on one of the couches, tips his head back, falls asleep. Wish I could sleep.

EIGHT DAYS EARLIER

Ivy

I hear dogs barking but ignore them. Christ,

there's a banging in my head like a fist against a door as the dogs break into another frenzied round of barking. I swear, if I had a gun, I'd shoot the hairy dumbasses. Shut up, shut up, shut up. I doze off. I'm a little girl again, watching my mom. She's covering a bruise on her cheek with concealer. Putting on red lipstick. "Men. Can't live with 'em. Can't live without 'em. You'll learn."

She holds me. Whispers to my hair, "Don't ever leave me."

I wake as if I'm coming up for air. Where the hell am I? Callie isn't in the bed. The clock on the wall reads eleven. There's Callie, shaking me, saying, "Oh my God, my parents. They'll expect me back, like, earlier. Get up, Ivy."

She's hopping about, throwing on clothes. It would be funny if everything didn't hurt. "Screw it, calm down, it's not even noon," I say.

She won't even look in my direction. "Just hurry up, Ivy. Please."

"What's really wrong?"

"I told you, I'm late." She still avoids my gaze.

"Are you being like this because I tried to kiss you?"

"No." She's blushing.

"Get over yourself." I say this gently, trying to joke, clear the air. "It's no big deal."

"It's a big deal for me," she says. Then she bursts into tears. "I'm sorry. I'm really sorry. I just really need to get home. My phone died and now we've slept in. Mom's going to be trying to get hold of me."

I get out of the bed. "She treats you like a little kid."

"I know."

I say, "It's not a bad thing. Growing up fast blows."

"Yeah — can we just go? Please, Ivy?"

I'm still dressed from the night before. I grab sunglasses from my bag. We head downstairs. I mumble, "I was only fooling around."

"Do you even remember?"

"Remember what?"

"What you said last night."

"What did I say?"

"About Isabel?"

"Oh, shit." What *did* I say? I put on my sunglasses.

Callie says, "Later. Everyone's already getting in Xander's car."

Xander nods a short hello to us. We're all quiet in the car. Callie watches out the window as we drive off. There's a stormy gathering of clouds on the horizon. We pull up at Callie's and she jumps out, hurries up the path. I get out my side of the car and watch her.

Her mom yanks open their front door. She's red in the face as she yells, "Where were you?" Uh, full on. She glances at me.

I hear Callie say, "I was . . . um." She's not making it any better. She just got out of Xander's car. If you're caught lying, it's time to switch to the truth.

Her mom bursts into tears. She says, "I couldn't call you, Callie. Last night she died."

Callie

For a moment I'm confused, remembering Ivy's story about Isabel. Then I realize with a sickening lurch that Mom's talking about my granny. Granny's dead. My mouth tastes bitter.

"No," I say.

"What were you doing with Ivy? I forbade you to see her. Whose car is that?" She pulls me into the house. Her grip is tight. The house is too warm. She says, "Where did you go? Who was driving that car? Why didn't you answer when I called?"

"The battery doesn't last long on this. I've been telling you I need a new phone."

Her eyes brim and she looks like a young child. "I called Rebecca's house. Woke them all up."

"I'm sorry, Mom. And I didn't mean to say that about the phone. I should have charged it before I left. I'm sorry I lied. I went to a party with Ivy. I didn't mean to lie to you, I just knew you'd never let me go if I asked and I didn't know we were spending the night and now I wasn't here when Granny died—" It hits me. It seems impossible that Granny's not here anymore. Her whole life, all the moments that made it, all of it over. I start to cry.

Mom softens, tells me it's okay, hugs me, but I know she's upset about the party, about Ivy. Worse—she's *disappointed*.

I whisper into her hair, "I wish I hadn't gone, Mom. I'm sorry."

It's enough for the moment. There are things to

organize. Mom draws me into the house and we are swept into a blur of family visits, and the endless details of a funeral, which is rapidly arranged for three days later, on Sunday. We discuss flowers and music, who will speak, the order of service. Mom and I select the coffin.

I'm helpful, sweet, and Mom doesn't mention the party, Ivy, my disobedience, her disappointment. Grief is like the ocean. It rushes over me in waves, sometimes knocking all the air out of my body with the force of memories, and then there are lulls when I feel fine, like nothing is wrong.

As the days hurtle by, Ivy calls loads, being supportive and endlessly kind, offering to come over, offering to help. But I don't see her. I don't see Rebecca either. She texts and calls. At least we're not annoying each other anymore. I don't go to work and Ana is understanding. I cocoon with my family until the funeral, which is held in a bleak room with a photograph of my grandmother at the centre, surrounded by heaps of roses. The smell is intense, sickly even. I can't believe a life ends like this, ushered out by strangers in dark suits. Rebecca's there. Ivy's there, wearing a black dress.

It's the first time since she returned that I've seen her in anything other than white and the first time with no makeup. Her eyelashes are pale and her skin is blotchy. She waves at me.

Granny is far away from me, her voice difficult to recall. Bouquets of roses, roses stacked up all over the place. I breathe in. Now the air smells like her and for a too-brief moment it's as if she's talking to me. *Careful, Callie.*

After the service, Ivy comes up to me and takes my hand. But I don't get to talk to her because one of my great-uncles is pulling me into an over-friendly hug and telling me what a lovely young woman I have become. Ergh. Old people kiss me on the cheek and tell me stories about my grandmother, stories that I hardly hear.

It's the day after the funeral, four days since the party. My relatives have left and I'm feeling empty and sad when Ivy texts and asks me to go for ice cream. I go to my mom's office and say, "Mom, can I, um, could I go out with Ivy, please?"

Mom raises her gaze and regards me steadily. "I saw her at the funeral."

"She's important to me, Mom."

"We haven't talked yet about the party. About you seeing her when I asked you not to."

"I know."

"You lied to me, Callie."

"I'm sorry."

"I don't want you to lie to me again."

"I'm really sorry." Tears spill from my eyes. "I couldn't tell Ivy that you wouldn't let me see her."

She spins her office chair slightly from side to side. "I know I should be more open-minded."

Embarrassment seizes me. "Do we have to talk about this?"

"Callie, I should be . . . I just don't want to see you hurt again."

"Mom, I really don't want to talk about this. Really."

"It's fine to—"

"Can we stop now? Please?"

She opens up her laptop and we both wait in excruciating silence. She says, eventually, "If she's your friend then I should try again with her. I know I should, so tell me, where do you guys want to go?"

"Just for a walk. We might get ice cream, something."

Mom takes another moment. "Okay," she says finally. "But no more lies."

"I promise," I say.

When I get to the ice cream parlour, Ivy gives me a huge hug, then says, "Ice cream. It's the only thing."

"Sure."

"Not mint-chocolate though."

"But it's my favourite."

"It always was." She buys us pistachio and mango ice cream. Sounds disgusting, but tastes delicious. I think about my granny and the quiet determination in her pale eyes, the way she circled her thumbs one over the other.

Ivy puts her arm around me and says, "I know how hard it is."

I lean in to be comforted. Ivy smells good, like she always does, that vanilla perfume.

She murmurs into my hair, squeezing me tightly.

She says, "I wish I could make it better," and I hear a note of regret in her voice.

I assume she must be thinking of her own loss, of her friend Isabel. I feel like I'm suddenly an adult, grown up in a way I don't want to be, and I long to be a kid again, free and easy.

We sit on the wall outside the ice cream place and swing our legs. Two spoons. One tub. That kid-feeling I just longed for rising up through me.

Ivy says, "Mom's being . . . Christ, I'm sorry to bring this up. You've got your own stuff . . . going on."

"No, I could do with something else to think about."

"I had a rough morning."

"With her?"

"Yeah. She was, you know, drunk again." Ivy pauses. "Why did you tell your granny about that day by the river?"

"I just said your mother was . . . I didn't go into details. Not about that. I was upset. It was pretty awful."

"Mom freaked out. Told me we were leaving and I didn't even have time to get my clothes, let alone think. She wouldn't let me call you or see you, say goodbye, nothing."

Our ice cream is melting. I lick mine quickly.

She says, "It was . . . after that living with her
was . . . at first, well, it was day to day. Mom
stopped drinking. I honestly thought she was done.
You know. She'd gone further than before. I mean,
trying to kill herself. The drinking didn't seem so
normal anymore. Does that even make sense? She
really tried. She did. She still had stacks of money
from her inheritance.

"We lived in a tiny place called Plato for a
while—I told you, remember, about Riley? The
son of her boyfriend—the one who wanted me to
strip for him? Then we lived with some developer
guy in San Francisco. Then she met Mark. Found
a new place to live: Kansas City. It's fricking hor-
rible there, but whatever.

"Six months after we arrived I found her passed
out in the bedroom. I tried to hide it from everyone
because she insisted she'd stop drinking for good.
Next time. Next time. She's really really good at hiding it. But, eventually, Mark found out." Ivy stares
off at a distant, invisible point. "I've been to so many
different schools I can't count them, but she won't
stop drinking. She can't stop. Nothing works. Mark

told her to get the hell out. Then, I found her on the bed. You know. Again. She was hospitalized. I was the only one who visited her. Things got a little out of control . . . For me, I mean."

"God, Ivy."

"Mom decided we had to leave Kansas City and she connected with Kevin so we came back here . . ." She pauses. "The worst of it? I just keep wondering if I'm going to end up like her."

"Of course not. No way."

"Alcoholism runs in the blood. I even look like her." She says, "I'm just really grateful you're here for me."

"I . . . I care about you, Ivy."

"Me too."

I have to go into work in the afternoon. I so don't feel like it, but I missed the last two shifts because of the funeral. When I arrive in the main gallery, Kurt's staring at the painting that's black all over, with the woman in white collapsed in the bottom corner, the one that reminds me of Ivy's mom.

Kurt's shoulders are hunched up like he's having a bad day too.

He must sense me beside him because he turns and says, "Haven't seen you around."

"I thought you might have heard."

He furrows his brow. "No, what's wrong?"

"It's just . . . My granny died the night of the party." The words are sticky.

"I had no idea. Sorry."

"Thanks. Ivy didn't tell you?"

"No. I haven't seen her." He steps back from the painting. "I—yeah. Forget it. I'm no good at this stuff. Maybe you want to work on that piece for *Flat Earth Theory* on the Surrealists." He quickly begins to backtrack, "Not if it's too soon, but—"

"No, I will."

"I always find working on something makes it . . . yeah . . . makes things easier."

"You know what? Remember the profile on my granny? Maybe I could do a series of those too, like, do some more interviews with other grandparents."

I hear my boss, Ana, coughing, um, not so discreetly. "Callie, whenever you're ready . . . I've got a zoo in here."

❉

The next morning, I lie around in bed, toying with a line in my head: *Light bursts like juice from a dropped carton, light splatters, stains, seeps into the cracks*. I hear Ivy yelling from the street.

"COOOO-EEEEEEEE, CAAAAAAA-LIIIIIIEEEE. TIME TO GO JOGGING."

I put the pillow over my head.

"CAAAALLLLLLIIIIIEEEE!"

I shove the pillow away, lurch up and look out the window. She's standing outside, yelling.

"Come down!"

"It's too early."

She stops, takes out her phone. A text pops up: **Never too early!**

I yell down, "Okay, okay. I'm coming."

I go to grab Mom's Zumba pants. Mom, Cosmo and Dad are all piled up in my parents' bed. I look at the three of them together. Mom wakes and blurrily lets me borrow the pants, telling me we should get some new ones for me to wear if I'm going to keep up with jogging.

—Down in 2 mins. Don't sing!

When I get outside, it's already warm. Golden light intercuts the street with bright stripes. There's something in the air, which I can only describe as the smell of *green*. I jog over to Ivy, who is bouncing foot to foot in a Lycra all-in-one short suit.

"How you doing?"

"All right."

Ivy says, "A jog will wake you up." She bounds off. I try to catch up, but she's too fast. She keeps going and looks back at me over her shoulder. "Race you to the river."

I run with determination, thinking about my granny, missing her. Ivy might be naturally faster and fitter, but I pummel the street, ignoring the ache in my chest and the burning sensation in my lungs. I soon hear Ivy puffing with her own effort.

Still, she beats me. We stop at the point where the road meets the riverbank. She's laughing, high, and already no longer breathless. I feel like I might actually die. I collapse on the grass and spread out my arms, looking up at the sky. I suck in air and pant, sweat making me wet and disgusting. Ivy lies down next to me. She takes a shuddering breath and says, "Sometimes it seems really bad."

I turn to her. "I knew she was old, I mean, I knew one day we'd lose her, but I thought it would be later. Not . . . just like that," I say.

"Look, Callie, I don't know if it might make you feel better, but I have these podcasts that are really great."

"Podcasts? Like what?"

"You know, spiritual stuff. Uplifting. I was in a pretty dark place myself not so long ago."

"What do you mean?"

"I'm . . ." She props herself on one arm so we're facing each other. She says, "What would you think if I told you I tried to end it." She puffs out a breath. "I mean, like Mom. On purpose."

"You tried to *kill yourself?*"

Ivy flops back to stare at the sky and I stare at her. She says, "See—I told you it was dark. It's been really hard."

"Ivy, you should have called me."

She's not looking at me. "What? Out of the blue after so many years? Anyway, I'm much better now."

"Not so many years." I pause. "You were really important to me. I really missed you." I want to ask

her how she did it, what happened, but I realize
she's starting to cry. I say, "Poor you."

"No way. I'm not going there. Not poor me.
Strong me. Powerful me. Everything-is-possible
me." She jumps up, brushes away her tears and
bounces from foot to foot. "Wanna race back?"

EIGHT

JULY 31ST

Kurt

I drum my fingers on the arm of the sofa. Regret is a strong drink. Whisky. Seeping through my veins. I'm drunk on it. The first night, Ivy whispered to me, "You make me feel safe."

What's a guy supposed to do with that? Her hair smelled good. Her hands were swift, light over my chest. She had that look of the Little Match Girl— that story of the kid dying to sell her last match. Desperate. Feisty. But it wasn't hard to shake any interest I had in her — all I had to think about was my birth-mom, her friends, *that* life.

Callie's friend from school hustles along the hospital corridor and rushes up to Xander, who rubs his face hard, sits up, acts like he was awake the whole time. She's small and muscular, with blue hair. Her makeup is smudged like she just got out of bed.

"I'm Rebecca Lane, remember me?" she says. "It doesn't matter. How can we find out stuff? Surely someone will tell us something. Where's everyone else? I just saw the car online and figured to come here. This is insane, Callie and I are fighting, it's all my fault, I was so jealous of Ivy. And now this. I can't believe it. I was so stupid . . . I wouldn't even listen to her."

"It's okay," Xander says.

"It's so far from okay. I have to find out what's going on." She leaves the way she came.

TWO DAYS EARLIER

Ivy

It's still dark when I wake. Mom and Kevin are shouting at each other. Their voices angry. I drift off, eventually. In my memory I'm three years old. In New York. Plush apartment. Dad yelling at Mom. She wears white: heels, dress, pearls. Her hair is gorgeous pretty. She's shrieking.

I put my hands over my ears. *Please stop crying.*

I hear Mom simpering, "I'm sorry, Kevin. It won't happen again."

Kevin seems placated because soon I can hear him grunting against her. I pull the pillow over my head. Fall back into a restless sleep.

I wake thinking about Callie. It was a good idea to tell her what I tried to do. I was sharing my pain, and pain shared is pain relieved. Once I've done my exercises, I call her.

"Want to meet at Toxique?"

"Morning. Wow, you really do get up early."

"So, wanna come shopping?"

"Sure. The place on Pine Hill? Next to the cup-cake store?" Callie says.

"Yeah. You walk past it all the time! So, I need a dress for BEneath tonight. You coming?"

"I can't. Mom won't let me."

What is it with her mom? I've always been so polite to her, sweet, interested in her books. "I have a question."

"What?"

"Does your mom still not like me?"

"It's not that, Ivy."

"What then? She's always been weird with me."

Callie pauses before saying, "She saw us —"

"What?"

"Um, when we were kids."

"So? Kids experiment."

"It wasn't . . ." Callie says softly. "It meant more than that. Anyway, she doesn't hate you."

"If you say so." Her mom makes out she's so in touch with young people, so sensitive, artistic, generous. "Thinking about her hating me makes me feel bad."

Callie says, "You shouldn't feel bad. It's Mom's problem, not yours. Okay?"

"Okay."

"You sure?"

"Yeah. And I'm sure I can figure out some way to get her to like me."

"Just give it time. I've been thinking about what you told me . . . about what happened. When you —"

"That's behind me now, Callie."

"Just, well, just promise me if you're feeling, I dunno, bad, you'll tell me."

"I'm feeling great. Remember, new town, new life."

"Okay. Well . . . I'll see you at noon."

"See you soon," I say.

I sit in front of my mirror. My face looking back at me is tight, my jaws tense, my cheeks flushed. What is with Callie's mom? What's her fricking problem? It's not like it was all my fault, but of course it couldn't be that her *perfect daughter* did anything — right? It couldn't be that her perfect daughter was the one to kiss me first. I release my jaw. I think of a bath draining, the dirty water swirling away. I say again and again, *I'm beautiful, I'm worthy.* Slowly I believe it.

Callie

Ivy and I arrange to meet at the clothing store. I get off the phone and lie back on my bed. I'm only just waking up. I play with the idea of actually writing down a poem but the lines are slippery and they swim away before I can catch them.

Mom and Dad ask me if I'd mind babysitting for the morning. I haven't really done that for them before, except for the day when Granny fell, and they seem nervous, instructing me not to use my phone, not to leave Cosmo unattended. When they're gone, I give him a bottle. He gobbles it down, then spits up so I put him in the bath, and he coos when I lightly splash him with water. After his bath, I dry and dress him again, and he settles in my arms and falls asleep while I tell him a made-up story about a girl who can fly.

My cell rings and I hurry to answer without waking Cosmo. It's Rebecca.

"What's up?"

"Not much," she says. "Tilly emailed. She's in love with some park ranger."

I whisper, "Hot."

"For sure. Why are you whispering?"

"Cosmo's asleep in my arms."

"Your brother? The one you don't like?"

"I do too like him."

"So you should. He's sweet. So, we didn't really get to talk at your granny's funeral. You doing okay?"

"I guess."

"Your granny was the best. I loved her story about your grandad meeting her at the station wearing a checked shirt—she told him he looked like a farmer. He laughed and told her that was *exactly* what he was. She said it was something they laughed about for years."

"I miss her," I say.

"I saw Ivy at the funeral."

"Yeah. About Ivy . . ." I say. I imagine Rebecca settling into the window seat she has, her bare feet tucked up, an open sketchbook next to her.

She says, "I'm the one with the problem."

"No. It's my fault too."

"'Kay. It's totally your fault too."

I laugh.

She says, "Is Ivy back for good then?"

"Hopefully."

"I suppose I'll have to hang with her then."

"She's had a really difficult time, Becs. She could do with friends right now."

"Right."

"Tell you what, we're going to Toxique in about an hour to buy clothes. Come with us."

She sighs.

"Come on."

"I can't . . . today. But maybe next time."

"What's wrong?"

"It's just Toxique isn't really . . . my scene."

"Have you ever even gone inside?"

"I've gotta go, Callie. I'll call you tomorrow." She ends the call before even saying goodbye.

I want to bang my phone against the coffee table, but it would wake Cosmo. "Wow, baby," I whisper, "life has gotten very complicated."

Ivy's waiting at the front door of Toxique. She waves when she sees me, and hugs me tight as soon as I'm within reach.

"Your mom was okay with you meeting me then?"

"She's fine. Anyway, sorry I'm late. Mom and Dad left Cosmo with me and only just got back."

"No problem."

"Maybe you should come over sometime and we could, well, you and Mom could get to know each other better."

"It's not like she hasn't spent time with me."

"True, but we were different then." I wonder as I say it how different we were then, how different I actually was. I have a flash of memory: the first time I tipped Ivy's face down to meet mine and found myself flushed with need, desire, fear. I was so bold.

I follow Ivy into the store. I've never been in before. It's small and boutiquey, way too expensive for me. The clothes are tiny, beautiful things, all lacy and delicate. Almost like underwear. The whole place smells of lavender and there's busy jazz playing.

I run my fingers over a pair of silver high heels, then I spot the price tag and step away. Ivy grabs them.

"They are perfect. Thanks, Callie, great eye. Along with my dress, these will knock everyone out at BEneath tonight."

"I wish I could come with you."

She turns to me and pouts. "What? You really can't come? But you have to."

"BEneath is out of the question."

"What if I come over and talk with her?" She kicks off her shoes and pops on the heels.

"She let me come hang out with you today but she'll never let me go to a bar. That's not to do with you, that's just how things are. Anyway, Kurt will be there with you."

"Yeah, about him. Or not. He's been— I guess since that party, well . . . he's not really been calling."

"No? I thought you guys were starting something."

"Yeah, go figure." She pulls a face.

"That sucks."

"That's why I need the perfect dress—like this. Then he'll realize what he's missing. No more of his 'let's just be friends' crap."

"He said that?"

"He doesn't mean it." She shimmies with the dress in her hand and I remember how she shimmied across the room wearing only underwear.

I follow Ivy to the back of the store. The sole

staff member, who is dressed like she's in a sci-fi movie, opens the door of the change room. Ivy slips in carrying the dress, leaving her purse with me. I step away to admire a rack of beautiful sparkly dresses. Dresses I would never, ever own. I find myself imagining Ivy getting changed, taking off her dress.

From inside Ivy's bag, I hear her cell ringing. I reach in to grab the phone, intending to pass it to her. Then I see the call display on the screen. *Isabel Cabezas*.

Isabel's *dead*. Ivy told me so.

I answer the phone.

A girl's voice says, "Ivy?"

"Isabel?" I whisper. "Isabel Cabezas?"

"Who's this?" The voice is sharp.

"Um, I'm a friend of Ivy's." I add, "I don't really understand. She said—"

"Tell her to send back my purse." I think of the identity card in my jean pocket. Isabel's identity card. The girl—Isabel—says, "She called Diego again last night."

"Diego?"

"Tell her to stay the fuck away from my boyfriend."

Ivy calls from the change room. "Callie, are you there?"

I whisper, "I have to go," and end the call, my mind racing. I shove the phone back into the bag and head over to see Ivy emerging, looking fantastic.

She does a full twirl. I make the right noises, but can't stop thinking about what I've just heard. I shudder as if I have been speaking to a ghost. I thought the girl was dead, Ivy told me she was dead, but now, there she was, full of life at the end of the line.

I interrupt Ivy's fashion show with a lie. "Um, my mom just called. I have to go. I'm sorry. And I really can't make it tonight."

"Callie, please come. I need you."

"I really have to go." *Isabel's alive. You lied to me. You told me she was dead.*

She picks up her bag and checks her phone. "Did you answer that?" she says.

"No" pops out of my mouth.

"Don't lie to me," Ivy says. "I can see from the call log you did."

"Ivy, I'm just . . . it's . . . kinda hard to . . . It was *Isabel.*"

"And? That makes it okay to lie?"

"Ivy"—I steady myself against a clothing rack—"you told me she was *dead*." My voice drops as I say this last word.

A long pause follows. I can't read Ivy's expression at all. Then she says, "When did I say that?"

"What do you mean *when*? At Kurt's party."

"What did I say?"

"You told everyone that Isabel died when you guys had a motorbike crash, that she died in your arms."

Ivy laughs. "That's crazy, Callie. Isabel isn't dead. She's . . ." Ivy catches my look and becomes more sombre. She says, "I was *drunk* at the party. And stoned. I was probably trying to be funny, or cool, or something."

"You said—"

"She didn't *die*. Whatever. I don't know what I said. I'm being honest now, really, and you have to trust me. Diego was the one who lit candles. He was sweet, and kind, and he loved me. And then Isabel stole him."

"She said he was *her* boyfriend. She said you gotta send her purse back, and stay away—"

"Isabel's twisting it to make herself feel better. You've never even met her, but you *know* me. Why would you listen to her?"

I weigh her up. I'm making too big a deal out of this. I've just been feeling so weird around Ivy today. Not myself.

Ivy says softly, "You *know* me, Callie. I was just high. Please?"

I nod. "It was really weird talking to her."

"I bet."

"No more secrets, 'kay?" I say.

She gives me a funny look, but it's gone so quickly I can't be sure it was ever there. She says, "Definitely no more secrets."

After the shopping trip with Ivy, I spend the rest of the day home sorting through photos of Granny. I notice how, when she was young, Granny and I were identical: same jawline, same slight awkwardness, same eyes. And I notice something else: Granny was really pretty.

I check my phone to find a message from Kurt:

Wanna go over ideas for the profile pieces?

Mom comes into the room, so I don't text back. She passes me Cosmo and I jiggle him up and down while he reaches chubby baby fingers clumsily to my mouth. He tilts his head to try and catch my eye. I look at him and he breaks into a wild smile. Who knew I was so funny!

Dad arrives home and insists we have a family movie night. We always have to watch non-violent, animated things because Mom and Dad don't want to distress Cosmo, although he's so tiny I'm not sure he can even see the TV. I sit there, pretending to enjoy the film, the three of them nestled on one sofa, me alone on the other. I think of Ivy getting ready to go to BEneath, then, as it gets later, I imagine her making her spectacular entrance.

The movie finishes and Dad says, "I thought the name of the muse of poetry and storytelling was a perfect name for my daughter, but I'm not sure now."

"What?"

"Calliope was wise and honest and brave. The wisest of the Muses . . . but maybe I should have named you after a main character instead, like —"

"Let's not spoil the evening," Mom says, putting a hand on his arm. She must have caught the look on my face.

He pulls her close to him. "Whatever you say, lovely. Gimme a smooch."

The rest of my family go to bed so I head to my room and find myself thinking about a fly trapped in a house. In my head I juxtapose the word *jagged* with the word *flight* and I think about the phrase *letting your guard down*. The lines are turning into a poem, maybe. I rifle through my desk. If I find a blank sheet of paper, I might *actually* write. Instead, I come across an old photo of Ivy and me. It's the same one she had in her room, the one of the two of us hugging, and I can see in my expression that I'm completely happy, almost unrecognizably so. As I look at the picture, the poem slides from my mind to be replaced by thoughts about Ivy. The taste of her mouth, that vanilla smell of her hair, her smooth skin. Thoughts I haven't had for years. Thoughts I haven't let myself have for years. Thoughts I can't seem to stop now. I picture her in the dress at Toxique, her sadness when she told me about trying to kill herself. A little voice says from deep inside me, *Careful, Callie*. But it doesn't stop me thinking about Ivy trying to kiss me at Kurt's party. And didn't Ivy mention that things weren't really happening with Kurt? She tried to kiss *me* the night of his party; surely that means something? I could sneak out of the house, climb down the tree, be with her. But then I remember Mom's face when Granny died and I know I won't go.

I *can't*.

Except, I can't stay home either.

I slip on the silver dress that Ivy gave me. It skims my body, silky and luscious. My skin tingles as if a tiny spider is creeping along my upper thigh. I push open my window and throw a pair of low heels and my purse to the ground. They thud, one after the other, the contents of the purse spilling, and I listen for my parents or Cosmo, sure they must have heard, but the only sound is the soft breath of night, and then the rustle of the leaves as I haul myself out the window and climb down by the branches to land like a cat on the grass.

It's warm underfoot. The night is like a peach, fuzzy and delicious on my tongue. I slip on my heels and check I have Isabel's ID in my purse.

The idea of owning the ID card of a dead-not-dead girl creeps me out and I quickly tuck it back into my wallet. *Don't think about it. Just move.* Guilt slides into the space that the creepy feeling opened up and I glance back at my window. Mom would be so upset with me if she knew what I was doing. I walk away from my house, night and summer in my hair.

I walk a couple blocks, turn the corner and see BEneath up ahead. It feels like the witching hour, the time when everything and anything is possible. Music from inside thrums through the air. I stop in the shadows.

NINE

JULY 31ST

Kurt

Xander watches Rebecca Lane head down the hospital hallway. I drum my palms on my thighs, restless. I can't figure out how much time has passed—it could have been minutes, hours. I seem to have lost my phone, so I can't check. The world has stopped making sense.

I think again about my birth-mom at that party when I was trashed when I was fourteen. She saw me. Stared. Then she dropped the guy's hand.

Shoved her way over. Seized my arm. My birth-mom's a small woman but her grip was steady. She said, "Get your shit together, kid."

"You're a fine one to talk," I said, or something like that. I can't remember exactly, but I know it was hard to speak. My tongue was fat in my mouth. My buzz had levelled off.

I remember what she said next. Perfectly. "You're better than this, Kurt." From her neck she took a leather cord with a silver dollar dangling from it. Tied it around mine. "You're *better* than this."

"Whatever."

But her words stuck into me. And something shifted. I've worn the silver dollar ever since.

Xander rests his head on his hands. Like it's too heavy for his neck to hold it up anymore. I want to tell him it's all okay, but that's not true. Unlike my mom, I can't think of the right words to fix this. The right words don't exist.

TWO DAYS EARLIER

Ivy

I see the boys in the booth at BEneath. "Hey, Kurt, Xander, everyone."

Kurt says, "Hey. I thought you said Callie was coming tonight." He tips back his beer bottle to drink.

"Yeah, well, she can't make it . . ." Why's he asking about her? Maybe something happened between them at his party when I was high. Is *that* why he's not interested in me?

I take a slow breath. Jumping to conclusions is like jumping into fire. I head to the bar and come back with tequila shots. Fire one down. Hand out the rest. "Let's party," I say, and raise a second glass to my mouth. The drink burns my throat. I say in my mind: *I'm not like my mother. I'm just having fun.* I slide next to Kurt.

"So why are you asking about Callie?"

He shakes his head. "No reason."

I can tell that he's hiding something. It's happening again. Tears spring to my eyes. Crap. Guys hate that, girls getting weepy. I scramble for something to say and come up with "You know, I just wish I hadn't said anything about the whole Isabel thing."

"Sounded tough."

And although a second ago my plan was to tell him the truth about what I said to everyone at the party—not that I really remember—the plan changes. The way Kurt looks at me is so kind, so sympathetic, even tender, that I find myself saying, "You have no idea what it's like to lose someone you love." It's not exactly a lie. More tequila. I *should* just be honest, but he's focused on me now, listening. I whisper, "I need a cigarette." My eyes fill again.

"Sure. Let's go."

Outside I stand in the silvery light of the sign and he gives me a cigarette, lights his own. He blows a smoke ring. Then another.

The tequila must have gone to my head. The words come out of my mouth: "We could make it work, you know."

"I already told you, Ivy."

He turns his face away. That's when I see Callie in the shadows.

What's she doing here? She's after *Kurt*? Is something going on with them? No. She wouldn't do that to me. I know how to make this better — he liked kissing me last time. I reach up, turn his face toward me and kiss him lightly.

"Ivy," he says — and shakes me off. Actually *shakes* me off.

"It's okay, Kurt. Just relax."

"This isn't funny."

"Kurt, I really think we could work . . ." I can hear myself getting whiny. Clingy. Guys *hate* that.

He lets go, walks away, his shoes thudding softly on the sidewalk. I look over to the shadows, desperate, but Callie's gone too. My heart is torn into thousands of tiny pieces, ready to be chucked in the garbage. Why does this keep happening to me?

Callie

A few feet from the lineup of partygoers chatting and waiting to get into BEneath, Kurt talks to her. Ivy — golden hair, white, tight dress, sparkly heels, stunning. She turns briefly in my direction but I don't think she sees me. I'm hidden in the dark, watching them smoke. Kurt's gesturing, lifting a hand, lowering it, like he's explaining something. Ivy presses up against Kurt like a kitten. His hands shoot up as if he's shocked.

Her mouth is on his.

And as she kisses him, everything becomes clear. Oh God. I'm in love with Ivy, violently, horribly, incredibly in love. The feeling is so intense, I stumble back. And then I'm running away, to the safety of the tree, which will sweep me up to the haven of my house, where I wish I could go back to being ordinary, well-balanced, *normal* Callie, whose biggest problems were dealing with her parents being wrapped up in their new baby, and what novel to read next.

Ivy

When I get in from BEneath, Mom is sitting on the loveseat with Kevin. She says, "Ooh, late night then?"

I hardly lift my gaze.

She says fondly, "Just like I used to be." She giggles and waves me over. "Come sit, pudding."

"I'm kinda tired. It's late, like you said."

"Oh, Ivy, babe, just a few minutes. We have to talk. We've been waiting for you."

Kevin leans forward in his seat. "Ding dong merrily! Big news in the world of us."

"What?"

Mom shows me her hand. A hulking diamond glimmers on her fourth finger.

"Is that . . .?"

Kevin toots, "Glory be, she agreed to marry me!"

"Oh."

Mom says, "Don't you love the ring?"

I can't say anything. My head is spinning.

Her voice lowers dangerously. "Can't you just be happy for me? If you knew what I gave up for you— I could have been a model, but, oh no, I was pregnant and so I did the right thing. Not like your father—"

"Don't start, Mom. Maybe I had a bad night, huh?"

Kevin blurts, "Go to bed, young lady."

"What? You two don't want to hear about me?"

He says, "You're wrecking this for us."

"It's never your problem, right, Mom?" My hands are shaking.

"Shut up," she yells.

As I head upstairs I toss over my shoulder, "I can't keep doing this—I try and I try and I try but nothing ever goes my way."

I keep it cool until I get to my room. I draw the curtain and peel off my dress. I do fifty squats, then another fifty. Two hundred sit-ups. Seventeen push-ups. I'm sweaty but not broken. Eighteen. They won't break me. Nineteen. They won't. I drop down, my face in the carpet, the ridges pressed against my nose. And I know I can't push up off the floor this time. Not again.

ONE DAY EARLIER

Callie

The next morning, after having seen Ivy kissing Kurt at BEneath, I need to get out of the house. I tell Mom I'm going for a walk and I wander down toward the river, thinking about my granny, thinking about Ivy.

I cross the bridge, noticing the scattered

orange traffic cones, the hammered-in boards to block off the barrier, the temporary traffic lights, and a large sign reading: WHEN RED LIGHT SHOWS WAIT HERE.

I don't know where I'm going until I arrive at the gallery. I push open the door, feeling the air conditioning and the even cooler quiet within. I find myself in front of the painting of the woman in white slumped in the corner. I stare at it for a long time, realizing she now reminds me not of Ivy's mom, but of Ivy. Then I head out of the gallery and come to a stop, sit on a low bench—and I start to cry. I'm crying about Ivy and my ridiculous feelings for her, crying about my grandmother, my mother, the way I've been acting, everything.

I hear footsteps come across the grass. I see sneakers, jeans, hooded sweatshirt. Kurt. I'm a huge mess, tears all over my face, mascara probably everywhere. I wipe my face and say, "God, I'm so embarrassed."

He sits next to me. "What's wrong?" he asks.

"Everything."

"Like what?"

"My granny. Ivy. You guys. Last night."

"What?"

"Outside BEneath. I saw you with Ivy."

"You were there?" he says. "That wasn't what you think."

"She wants you. It's fine, I get it."

"You've got it wrong."

"I *saw* you."

"You saw *her*. Kissing me. I don't want her. I told her that." He puts his hand over mine. His palm is hot and clammy. His eyes are blazing.

A whole load of stuff clicks into place. Kurt trying to talk to me at the gallery, at his party. I say, "No, Kurt, that's not what I mean . . ." I move my hand away.

Kurt lets out a breath. "You're beautiful. And smart. And, yeah, I . . . I can't stop thinking about you." He adds, quietly, "I should have told you. Before. Ages ago. I should never have . . . with Ivy. Look, I tried to tell you at my house. You just shut me down, so I can't figure out if you're interested or not at all. Seeing you here, I just . . . I just had to tell you. Can't. Stop. Talking."

No way. This is all going wrong. A line pops into my head: *Words like river fish*. "It's not you . . ."

He nods. "I get it. I do. You think I'm not good enough for someone like you."

"Kurt! It's nothing like that."

"Sorry. I'm being — whatever. I get it."

"I'm not sure *I* get it anymore," I say. "See . . . it really is because of me, not you. I think I might be, well — "

"What?"

"Oh God," I say, my voice catching. I think about how three years ago Ivy kissed all along my stomach, her mouth pausing before she lifted herself to kiss my mouth harder. I think about Mom's face after Ivy left, when she told me she'd seen Ivy and me together. Mom was so angry. I say to Kurt, "Look, Ivy and I have a . . . a history. I guess I've been pretending to myself that it meant less than it did. I have to figure out a lot of stuff."

"A history?"

"Yeah. Like, well, we were more than friends. I guess."

He is very quiet. Then he says, "I was not expecting that."

"I'm just figuring it out myself."

"So . . . you're gay?"

"I don't know what I am. Maybe. Whatever I am, I have feelings for Ivy."

Neither of us says anything for a moment. I wonder if he's going to walk away, if what I've just told him makes him want to leave.

He says, after another pause, "That's cool. Surprising. But cool."

"It is?"

"Look, can we go for coffee now? Something. Talk about *Flat Earth Theory*?" He adds, "I'm not good at this stuff. Remember?"

I nod.

We head to the new breakfast café, sit down at a table and share a cinnamon bun with a cup of coffee each. I can't stop myself eating more of the bun than Kurt does, tearing off sticky strips and putting them one after another in my mouth. Kurt goes and buys another bun for us, and when he returns with it I say, "Sorry, it's just really good."

"Don't apologize. You shouldn't feel bad." And he's not talking about cinnamon buns.

"I don't know if I do feel bad. I'm just really confused."

"It explains a lot."

"Yeah? Like what? Like why I'm not interested in you?" I say it lightly and my awkward joke seems to cheer him up.

He smiles. "Exactly."

"Nothing's going to happen with me and Ivy. She's into you."

He shakes his head. "I'm not going there. At my party. When she was high. Too much like my birth-mom."

I brush aside his comment. Instead, we talk about the conclusion to my article, that the name — Redmen — of our football team is dated and racist. Kurt likes the way I explored all the angles and asked "tough questions." I say, "Ego boost. Thanks."

"You're a good writer. You know that. Don't you?"

"Sort of. 'Kay, let's talk about something else."

Kurt walks me home. As we get to my doorstep, my cell rings. It's Ivy.

I glance up at her house and there she is at the window, staring down at me. She's wearing white and she looks like a ghost. I raise my hand to wave.

Kurt says, "Answer that. I should go anyways. But my dad's bringing me into the city tomorrow — he's gotta get the car fixed. I could swing by here. Go over the ideas for the profile pieces. We covered a lot . . ." He scratches the back of his head and smiles. "But not the profile pieces."

"Okay, great."

As soon as I answer my cell, which is still ringing, Ivy says, "Come over?"

I don't know if I want to see her right now. I think of her face as she leaned to kiss Kurt last night. I wish she would look at me like that, but it's not going to happen. It didn't mean anything to her three years ago. I need to get my head straight.

"I've been out all morning — I'm kinda tired. How about tomorrow?"

"Sure." I can't make out her expression through the glass.

I wave at her again, but then images of the two of us together fill my head. I say, "I gotta go."

TEN

JULY 31ST

Kurt

Ivy's mom appears alone at the end of the hallway.
Rushing. Shouting, "It's good news." She shakes
Xander awake. "Ivy's come around. I've seen her."

Xander waits.

I wait.

Something's not quite right.

Xander says, "Any news about Callie? She was in
the car."

Thank God he's asked.

Ivy's mom is quiet. Then she says, "They haven't found Callie, Xander. I thought you knew that. She's not at the hospital."

Callie. She's not here.

ONE DAY EARLIER

Ivy

I wave down at Callie through the window as I talk to her on my cell phone. What was she *doing* with Kurt two minutes ago?

I say, "Come over?" I take a deep breath. Fill myself with light.

"I've been out all morning—I'm kinda tired. How about tomorrow?" She sounds tense.

"Sure." I wait for her to mention Kurt. She doesn't, but she gets off the phone fast. When she's gone inside, I stay at the window, lean my head against the glass.

I know what I saw. I've seen it before, back in Kansas City, watching Diego holding another girl's hand. I tried to tell myself there was some explanation. But they were walking too close together. She lifted her mouth to kiss him. And then I knew it wasn't the first time.

I loved him. I loved my dad too. Until he left my mom, moved to Paris to live a beautiful life. He told me once that he had known things were *never* going to work out with Mom. She was drinking before he left. But I knew he was lying.

The window is cold. I'm cold in the thick of summer. I shiver.

Callie and Kurt. There's an explanation. I call her back, ask, "What was Kurt up to?"

"Kurt? Talking about the zine. I ran into him by the gallery."

See. An explanation. I let her words seep through me. Nothing's wrong. Everything's fine. Except, I can't stop shivering.

JULY 31ST

Callie

It's the last day of July and my room's so hot I have to escape downstairs. "Wow," I say to Mom, who is slicing a mango on the cutting board, "there's no way to breathe up there."

She nods. "Your father and I were talking about air conditioning. It's expensive, but on days like this it feels worth it."

I reach across the counter and pop a piece of mango into my mouth. "Yum. So, Kurt would like to come over later, to talk about an article."

"Here? Okay, sure. Now, Kurt—" She raises an eyebrow. "You've mentioned him a couple of times. Is he interested?"

"Sort of." I add, "But I'm not. We're just friends."

There's a long pause. In *The Odyssey*, the sailors steer the ship away from the monster Charybdis, who swallows down the waters of the sea. But I can't steer the ship anymore. I *can't* go on like this. I pour myself a coffee, add sugar and some cream. As I shut the fridge, I say, "Mom, I know you don't like it but you have to . . ." I try again. "See, it might be . . . there might not *be* a guy for me, if you get what I mean."

She leans against the other side of the counter and puts down the knife.

I continue. "What happened with Ivy in the past, well, I *like* her. Now. I mean. And even though she's into guys and nothing's going to happen with us, no matter what I might think sometimes . . . in the future, well, I just don't know that I'm that interested in boys."

She says, slowly, "You and Ivy . . . you were too young to be . . ."

I choke up. "I don't know if I'm gay or not gay or what, I just don't know, but pretending like this doesn't exist is killing me."

She nods, but doesn't speak.

"Not that it matters. She's not interested . . . like that . . . in me."

"Oh, honey, I'm sorry I've been so . . ." And Mom starts to cry. "I guess it's been hard for me, when I've been busy with Cosmo, to see that you're growing up."

"You were so angry with me and Ivy."

"Because you were young. And because I suppose I just wonder if you want to be *with* Ivy or if you want to *be* her."

"However you say it, doesn't change how I feel."

"I wouldn't have you any other way." She comes round the counter and kisses me on the top of my head. "Whatever you choose."

I'm steering past the churning waters as she says it. The black whirlpool of fear — Charybdis — behind me, if he ever existed. The ocean has opened out, wide, blue and full of possibility.

My phone buzzes. It's Ivy: **U coming to Xander's party 2nite?**

—**I don't know . . . first I've heard of it!**

—**wanna ride?**

—**what car?**

—**u'll see.**

—**I don't know if I can go yet!**

Kurt arrives at four and we sit around in the kitchen, drinking tea. Mom clearly likes that he can talk to parents. Both Tilly and Dahlia always find it hard to hang out with my parents.

Eventually Kurt says, "So, what's the plan. Are you going to Xander's?"

Mom turns to me, quizzically.

I say, "I, um, figured the answer would be no, so I didn't ask."

Mom holds my gaze. "It might be time for me to

surprise you, honey." She turns to Kurt. "Are you going?"

He nods. "Xander and I are pretty tight."

"What's he like?" Mom asks.

"Xander? Smart. Responsible."

She laughs. "You're just saying what I want to hear."

"Callie can look after me," he jokes, "if that's what you're worried about."

Mom laughs again. "Well, I guess if Xander's a good kid, you can go, Callie."

"Really, Mom?"

"I want you home by midnight." She adds, "Soon we should go out for lunch, you and me."

"Sounds good."

"Right, I've got to do some work. You two okay with Cosmo?" Mom passes Cosmo to me, and heads upstairs to her office.

I jiggle Cosmo on my knee. He burbles. I say to Kurt, "Ivy offered me a ride."

"Mind if we walk?" he says. "I kinda want to steer clear for a bit."

"I feel bad. She offered."

"Okay then. We can ride with her. I'm a big boy."

I let out a long breath.

He says, "What?"

"I'll have to talk to her. Tell her how I feel."

"You're going to, then?"

"I want her to know. But maybe you and I should walk; it'll be easier to tell her when I see her at the party. In person."

Kurt plays with Cosmo while I text Ivy to tell her we don't need a ride.

ELEVEN

JULY 31ST

Kurt

The walls of the hospital waiting room are too close. Ivy's mom repeats herself to Xander. "They haven't found Callie, Xander. She never made it to the hospital."

I speak, my voice unsteady. "Where is she?"

No one answers me.

It's as if I'm not here.

I say it again, louder. "Where is she?"

Neither of them turns around.

Pain radiates from my chest to my hands. There is a roaring in my head, a whoosh of understanding. *They don't hear me.*

Ivy

The night of Xander's party, I'm in my new red car. My hands are on the wheel, leather beneath my fingers. My nails are violent red. The air is warm on my lips. Music makes the whole vehicle vibrate — it's Isabel singing. I can't stop listening to her — I keep replaying her songs at home, and now in the car. I tried to pretend to Callie that it was me singing this. Some joke. Isabel's song creeps through my body with a tingly feeling, like someone's running a finger up my spine. The car idles, purring beneath me. My mouth is too tight to smile.

Callie texts: **Gonna walk — lovely day. I'll meet u there. Can't wait xxx.**

I saw Kurt go into her house around four. I know how this plays out. Her text is pure confirmation. So when Callie and Kurt leave Callie's house, I'm waiting.

"Hey, gorgeous," I say to Callie. I can hold this together. There's light in my heart. They *must* have another explanation. They'll tell me when they get in the car and everything will be fine, just fine.

Callie says, "No way, nice car!"

Kurt stands there, stiff, awkward. I can see it in his face—he wants Callie. I want *him*, and Callie's standing there with him like it doesn't matter at all.

I say, "Kevin bought it for Mommy dearest and me. They're getting married, you know."

Callie says, "Cool—" She's not meeting my eye.

"I posted a photo of it online—I'm not Kansas Pearl anymore, just Ivy Foulds. Everyone will have seen it by now—they're going to be climbing over themselves to be my friend."

"It's really nice." Callie's acting like nothing's wrong. Like it's *okay* that she's stolen Kurt from me. *No, stay calm, Ivy, stay focused.*

"Come on, get in, it's brand new. It even smells new, it's, like, delicious. We can drive as far as we like, no one would even notice, and get out of this craphole. Or we can just go over to Xander's party."

Callie says, "Mom wants me back by midnight."

"Like Cinderella," I say.

She smiles, looking pained.

Kurt's staring at me like I'm a snowstorm about to turn into a blizzard. But at the same time, he wants to please Callie. Puppy dog. All men are puppies.

I say, "Let's go."

Kurt says, "Let's go."

Both of them get into the car.

Callie

Kurt, like a gentleman, sits in the back seat and I climb into the front. I'm close enough to smell Ivy's perfume. Her hand almost brushes my thigh as she puts the car into reverse to back out of the space. She shifts to drive, her hand moves away and my mouth goes dry with longing.

Ivy drives toward Xander's house, which is on the other side of the river. She's quiet, as if she's looking for words. Then she says, "Callie, Kurt was my boyfriend. I need some sort of explanation—"

Oh, wow. I scramble to say, "We're just *friends*, Ivy. Kurt and I have been friends for ages."

"Isabel said the same thing. At first."

"Callie and I *are* just friends," says Kurt. "She's not interested."

"But you are."

"God, this is all ridiculous." I force a smile. "What tangled webs we weave."

Ivy says, "What's that supposed to mean?"

"This isn't the time."

"You'd better tell me, Callie."

"It's nothing to do with Kurt. Look, can we just talk about this later?"

"Tell me now."

My cheeks grow hot. "No. Not now."

"So there's no explanation for Kurt being at your house?"

I say in a rush, "I like *you*, Ivy."

She says through clenched teeth, "If you like me, why didn't you want to kiss me? You turned me down."

"You were *high*," I say. "It wasn't the right moment. I was scared. And I didn't want it to be like that. It was never like that before—it meant something. At least it did to me."

"Don't lie to me! I know what you and Kurt have been doing."

"Ivy, calm down. This is a stupid misunder-standing."

"I understand all right."

"Stop yelling at me."

Ivy spits out, "I stole Isabel's motorbike. She was at the party with Diego—she was never on the bike with me. I drove it as fast as I could. I came off the road and hit a wall. Boom . . . On purpose."

"What do you mean 'on purpose'?" I'm sweating.

"That was how I tried to kill myself. Remember?"

Kurt says, "You tried to kill yourself?"

"I *wish* Isabel had been with me on the bike. Bitch. Then she wouldn't have ended up with Diego."

"How can you say that?"

"She deserved to die." She glances at me. Her eyes are glazed. "I don't believe you about Kurt. I'm not a fucking idiot."

"I never said you were an idiot. I think *I'm* the idiot."

"What does that mean?"

"I was starting to think I was in love with you, but maybe I don't even *know* you."

Ivy's words slur. "I'm just like my mom."

"Oh my God, Ivy. You're drunk. Stop the car!"

"I'm beautiful. I'm worthy. I'm full of light."

She steers onto the bridge.

Kurt yells, "Ivy, stop the car!"

She speeds up and turns to me in her seat, lifting her hands. She looks me full in the face and says, "*You* did this."

I grab for the wheel. She fights me off. Kurt undoes his seat belt and, from the back, tries to reach the wheel too.

The bridge. The construction. That sign: WAIT HERE—

The car slams into the damaged barrier and flies through the air as my left shoulder rips from the socket and Kurt's full weight smashes over me into the front windshield. *He undid his seat belt* . . . Then he crushes me against the airbag, which in turn crushes me from the front.

I can't hear anything, but I sense the car falling. The weight of Kurt shifts and now I can see. The sun is low in the sky, scorching the undersides of the clouds, tangling Ivy's hair in light, and we are plummeting, heavy as tombstones, heavy as last words.

We hit the water hard. Pain and sound and terror fill me, but I'm alive. The car sinks and cold, cold water pours in the windows, and in Ivy's door— which has flung open on impact.

The airbag presses on me and I struggle to undo my belt. I shove Kurt, and then try to pull him loose, free him.

Where's Ivy? There's no time to look.

We are mermaids, slippery, watery, drowning.

I have to save Kurt. I tug at him. It cannot end like this. Water is up to my collarbone. My throat. I fill my lungs with air, plunge under and turn Kurt so his face is toward mine.

Kurt

And now I remember.

Being in the car. Back seat. Ivy talking batshit crazy. The car hitting the barrier. Callie screaming. Flip. Smash.

I think of the way no one has spoken directly to me; even at the party I was ignored. I think of the way Mrs. Foulds stared at me blankly. I think of the second cup of coffee, the one I thought Xander brought for me in the waiting room. I think of the remote that I couldn't work.

Xander and Mrs. Foulds are still talking but the lights flicker. Strobe effect. Can't they see it? I stagger away from them, like a drunk.

Dead. That word. It plays over and over in my mind. A dull word, punctuated at both ends.

I'm dead.

The lights go off.

Callie

Things I remember, falling through my mind like leaves through the sunlight.

My mother typing at her desk, the tap of the keys.

My father sitting in an armchair in my bedroom reading *The Odyssey*.

Cosmo watching me, his eyes carefully focusing, his gummy mouth smiling.

Kurt. The way he scratches the back of his head when he listens to the things I say.

Ivy's mother, poised like an angel at the edge of the water.

I'm sitting on a branch of a tree, my feet dangling.

   I see the moving van two doors down, a green car, the passenger doors opening, a girl getting out.

   I see the back of her head before I see her face for the first time.

   I remember how I loved her, how she felt in my arms.

✳

All the days rush at me, every day I've lived, a photomontage of memories. There's Kurt standing outside my house in the evening sunshine. There's my father, leaning against my doorway, telling me a story, turning to kiss my mother. There's Cosmo grabbing at my finger with his podgy baby hand.

There's my mother, typing, music playing, concentrating. She sees me and so she pauses mid-sentence. She rolls back her chair and I come into the room. I'm crying and she's holding me, kissing my hair as I sob into her chest.

I wish I could tell her that I love her.

She releases me, looks in my eyes, love spilling over, and for a moment that look feels strong enough to hold me to her forever.

But I can't hold on.

I let go.

I'm soaring.

Ivy

Pain shoots through me.

Someone shouts, "She's hemorrhaging."

Callie. I'm sorry. Please don't leave me.

Callie

My granny stands before me and the air smells of rose petals, sweet, floral, edible. Behind her is nothing but sky and it's the prettiest thing I've ever seen.

I try to concentrate, try not to drift.

Words like river fish.

My granny says, "Oh, Callie."

I kiss her papery cheek. "I miss you, Granny."

"Don't stay here," she says. And she fades away as if she were nothing but air.

I call for her, but she's gone. Then I see Kurt walking along the riverbank, searching for something, maybe for me.

I run to him, shivering, and put a hand on his arm, which is cold, so cold.

"Kurt," I say, testing my voice.

"Where were you? I didn't know. A ghost of myself without even knowing." He sounds lost. "The lights keep going on and off."

"I had to swim. I had to leave you there," I sob. "Oh, Kurt. Did it hurt?"

"I don't know. I don't know how I got back here from the hospital. First, I thought I was at the party—I don't know how I got there. Then I was at the hospital, waiting. But I've been dead the whole time. Now I'm here."

"Hey, hey, shh. You're not making sense." I notice the silver dollar round his neck.

His eyes fix on mine. He says slowly, as if he's speaking through water, "I can't come back to my parents. My birth-mom. My brothers. I can't come back."

"Oh, Kurt, I'm so sorry."

"It's not *your* fault," he says, suddenly coherent.

"How could I have been so blind?" I say. "I sit around reading and rereading novels where people do terrible things, but in real life I float in a bubble."

"You couldn't fix her."

"I was so naive. Thought I was so grown up but I was just a—how could I have thought I was in *love* with her?"

"Shh, stop." He touches the letters of his tattoo.
"I got this after my birth-mom said something to
me. γνῶθι σεαυτόν — 'Know thyself.'"

"No way? From above the temple of Apollo at
Delphi?"

He says, "Geek. No one knows that stuff."

"I always wanted to go there — to the temple
and see into the future — when I was little. All that
prophecy stuff is cool."

"You really are a geek," he murmurs. He turns
serious. "I wish things had been different, Callie." He
adds, "There's a chance for you. Look." He points.

We both look at my body where it lies, pale,
washed up at the side of the river.

I whisper, "It's not fair. You don't deserve this."

"You need to hurry."

I think of my family, of my home, of the things I
want to do. I think about *Flat Earth Theory*, the poems
I want to write, the story I have to tell. "But I . . ."

"But nothing. Go."

I know he's right. I step toward my body.

He says, "I'm going to miss you, Callie."

My stomach hurts. My face, my neck too. I
reach up and feel my skin. It's wet. I'm lying on the
grass, the river beside me.

TWELVE

AFTER

Callie

I stir. My parents and my baby brother are in the hospital room. The three of them together.

"She's awake." That's my dad, yelling, running out to the corridor, shouting, "Nurse! Anyone? She's awake!"

My mom leans in to hold me, Cosmo squished between us. She's crying. I feel her tears through the shoulder of my hospital gown.

Later they tell me about Ivy. She survived the crash but hemorrhaged and died in the hospital. I wish I could talk to her, yell, scream, hate, forgive, but she's gone.

And then they tell me about Kurt. I knew, but the news is a shard of glass in my heart.

Later still, I tell the police what happened. I tell them everything. My mother is here, her head in her hands.

Mom holds me while I cry. There will be many more days like this.

The death of us
    Words slide through my head. I'm so tired.

✳

Rebecca arrives.

I say, "Um, you're not crying, are you?"

"I might be."

"You don't normally cry."

"Yeah, well," she says, "you don't normally go off a bridge either."

"I'm sorry for . . . everything," I say.

"You're sorry? You have nothing to be sorry for."

"I knew. Deep down. I knew Ivy was messed up. I just wanted . . . I guess you were right . . . I . . ." My voice drops. "I thought I was in love with her."

"You were."

Neither of us looks at the other.

Rebecca says, "I can't believe what she did."

I say, "I can."

Rebecca pauses. "When you get out of here, you—I—well, do you want to come to mine? Have that breakfast, or something?"

"Sure," I say. "Sure. That sounds really good."

✳

Days pass. Sometimes, when I wake, my parents stand jiggling Cosmo between them. One day, they give me a new phone. It's full of texts. More days pass. My friends visit; Tilly is back from the cabin, Alison and Alex from *Flat Earth Theory* stop by. It'll be time for me to go home soon. My body is healing.

Early one morning I open my laptop. I toy with the idea of writing some lines of poetry onto a blank page, lines that have been blooming in my head since the accident.

She asked you to stop by the river
  when the world cracked open like an egg.
The space you never filled, a water glass spilled.

Then I hear Kurt's voice: *I lean against a tree at the back of the yard, the night around me like black water.*
"Kurt?" I say into the dawn. "Ivy?"
In the silence, I listen.

Acknowledgements

Thank you:

Hadley (can I thank you twice?!)
Jackie
Maria
Allyson
Leona
Jen
Émile
Dad
Mum

and
above all

Yann

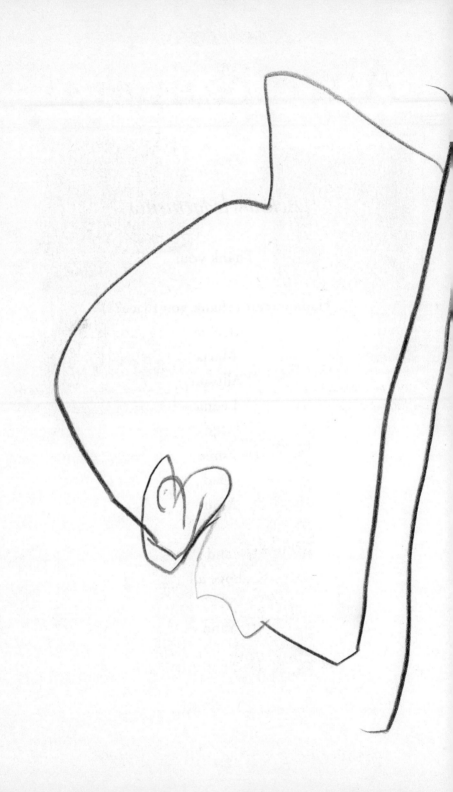

Also from
Alice Kuipers

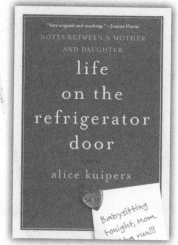

Winner of the Saskatchewan
First Book Award

Winner of the Arthur Ellis Award
for Best Juvenile/YA Crime Book

Winner of the Saskatchewan Book Award
for Young Adult Literature

alicekuipers.com | @AliceKuipers

WHAT'S NEXT?

Follow Frenzy for all the latest and greatest in YA books.

 @hccfrenzy  @hccfrenzy

 hccfrenzy.ca